# INVESTIGATION GREED

MEL TAYLOR

SEVERN 🖢 RIVER
PUBLISHING

Severn River Publishing
www.SevernRiverBooks.com

ISBN: 978-1-64875-559-0 (Paperback)

# ALSO BY MEL TAYLOR

**The Frank Tower Mystery Series**

Investigation Con

Investigation Wrath

Investigation Greed

Investigation Envy

To find out more about Mel Taylor and his books, visit

**severnriverbooks.com/authors/mel-taylor**

# 1

Lucas Park looked at the message on his phone and smiled, thinking he no longer needed to kill his wife. He tucked the phone into his pocket and walked past the leaking faucet he was supposed to fix six months ago, a broken table, four dead roaches, a pile of dirty clothes and two separate stacks of bills yet to be paid.

He stopped when he reached his wife, Joni Park. She wore a hat while inside the apartment and every few minutes pushed on the few strands of exposed hair, jamming the ends back up under the wool covering. "Ya look like you're going somewhere." Her jaw never moved, and the words seemed to escape from the chapped lips.

In his daydreams, Park saw himself soaking in the cobalt waters of the Bahamas, wavetops glistening like cut jewels. There would be people waiting on him on his own personal island with a massive cabana decked in marble and erected on the sand. He could just stay there all night, handing drinks to only special invited guests with great looks. And no Joni. Yes, he would and could do all these things if there was any truth to the phone message.

"Going out." Park had a sneer on his face as if he was hiding some secret deep within his heart. He was not a tall man, just a finger's width over five-feet-tall. He was bald except for the scrape of hair above both ears.

"Ya payn' the rent?" she asked. "Manager's threatening eviction again."

"I'm doing my best."

Her brow lines showed the worry in her face. "I work, you spend. I need some help! When are you ever going to have some money?"

Park's face resembled someone who had panned for gold and never found anything, only to finally discover a giant nugget in life. The sneer turned into a full smile, one that he could not control, the inner confidence was boiling up out of his gut, making it impossible to hold a calm detached expression. This was his one chance to turn around the misdeeds, the job firings, empty lottery scratch-offs, and finally move into the express lane. He took out the phone one more time to make sure he was reading the message correctly. Assured of his facts, Park turned the door knob wondering if his good fortune would mean he would never have to enter his wretched apartment again. "I'll be back in an hour," he said. And then he was gone.


"This has to be a joke." Cason Willow held up the phone message to his live-in girlfriend Sonia Mason. She pushed a shoulder-length growth of hair away from her face and studied the message. "Who is it from?" She shook her hair back with a hard snap of the head, never taking her eyes off the cell phone.

"I don't think I can pass this up." Willow had potato chip crumbs down the front of his shirt. He wore jeans designed with holes cut at both knees, a red-striped flannel shirt and no socks. When he stepped back, he knocked over a stack of books. "I can continue studying for my exam or I can go to this."

Sonia's large brown eyes moved to him. "How many people got this message you think?" The right side of her face was pushed up by the smile. "This just has to be a prank."

"Prank or not, I can't pass this up."

"And it says, 'don't come before 1:00 AM.' What if you came early?"

Willow grabbed Sonia's phone. "And you don't have a message like this?"

"Just you, sweet cheeks." She smacked him hard on the ass.

Willow sat down in the stack of couch cushions. The apartment was arranged in earth tones. Brown cabinets, beige couch, off-white throw rug, tan picture frames and a black table. Sonia looked serious. "Our student loans are eating us alive. If you fail this test tomorrow, you'll be out more money. The time to drop the class was two months ago. Have to do it over."

"But if this message is really true, who needs the class?"

He looked at her as if nothing she could say would deter him from going to the location. She had successfully stopped him from buying into a stock tip that sank on the third day of trading. Two years earlier, she got him to change his mind and not move to that city out west, the one hit by five forest fires in sixty-five days. And she once convinced him not to eat a suspicious dish and later found out everyone else got sick. Sonia Mason reached into her gut and ruminated until she had her conclusion. "I don't want you to go. Something tells me this is wrong."

"Are you kidding? I can't pass this up. I'm going." He leaned toward the door, letting his body language put a stamp on his decision.

"If you trust me, you'll stay home."

"You ever think you could be wrong, Sonia? Just once? I'll call you when I get there."

She heard the door close hard and then she was swallowed up by the silence in the room.


Pam Oakman always talked to herself. Somehow, she managed to make everyone come to her way of thinking, that the words directed at herself were a sign of genius. She liked to weave perfect lines of tied braids running from her forehead to the butterfly tattoo on her neck.

"Now, what do I do with this?" She pushed the phone away from her like it was a bowl of soup with a fly floating wings up in the middle. Pam went back to her world of buying and selling items. She had just closed up her consignment shop and she went about business as if she would never open the door again. She stacked a set of polo shirts in one corner, and rearranged a rack of dresses. Pam wiped a line of sweat off her brow and stared at the cell phone. She picked it up and again studied the message.

The message gave her four hours to be at the exact location. "This can't be right," she whispered to herself.

She put the phone down for the fourth time.

Pam stared at a picture of a teen on the wall behind the cash register. "I love you baby."

She turned off the lights to the place, took out her car keys and picked up the cell phone, bringing up the message yet again. When she locked up the door, the phone face was still bright like a beacon. She read the few sentences, then headed to her car. The words on the phone still fresh.

ALL THE MONEY YOU EVER WANTED. FREE

JUST COME. DON'T PASS UP THIS CHANCE.

1:00 A.M. NO EARLIER. STILTON BAY STREET AND THIRD AVENUE

IF YOU DON'T COME, SOMEONE ELSE WILL CLAIM THE MONEY

## 2

The cool reached into the pores of Stilton Bay, Florida, as the sun had moved down and melted into the horizon of the Atlantic hours earlier. The heat of the afternoon was also gone, making it easier to touch outdoor restaurant tables or stroll the wide concrete sidewalks. A row of cars lined up near the entrance to the city park at Third Avenue and Stilton Bay Street. Pam Oakman waited until twenty cars arrived before she got out. Cason Willow leaned against his sedan and surveyed the park. He didn't see anything resembling a stash of money.

There were perhaps thirty people, standing alone, yet together, like pieces of Stonehenge, no one daring to speak, hands in pockets, eyes staring in all directions, and no one ready to leave. The ocean was close, and the blended smell of brine and sun block wafted over the gathering.

"There's nothing here," Willow finally said in the direction of Lucas Park.

"You get the same message?" Park responded.

"We're all suckers." Willow started walking toward the deepening shadows of ten live oak trees. "Did anyone look for a sign? The person who started all this?" He kept walking to the large pavilion in the center of the park. The layout was small, and the park was a favorite for anyone taking a quick break before or after dealing with the warm sand. There was a mumbling in the crowd, as a few started to question why they even bothered to come. Six people stayed behind and inched toward their cars.

The park was a three-acre spread of palm trees and tough St. Augustine grass. All the founders of the city probably envisioned a mini Central Park. The outer rim of the park was lined with trees. Two earthen paths gave locals and tourists a quiet walk through the area. On the east, the park was open to the ocean. A wall of concrete and coral rock served as a barrier between the park and the sand leading to the blue Atlantic. The place was usually crawling with people sitting, hiking and others headed to the beach. Now, late at night, the popular spot was a bit on the haunting side.

"What is that?" Pam Oakman pointed to the central pavilion and something next to the community grill. She gave up on her slow stroll and broke into a run. Others followed her movement and soon more than ten people were jogging toward the find.

Willow reached the pavilion first. He stopped. Everyone who came next formed a line at the edge of the round structure. All eyes were fixed on what they discovered.

A body.

The man was on his back, arms outstretched and not moving. The folds and bends of his body did not look normal, like his clothing was stuffed with something.

"I'll check," Willow told the group. He walked up to the figure on the concrete. A bevy of bugs circled his face, dancing in the glow of the pavilion lights. Willow stopped again. He saw what was inside the man's shirt, pants and even his shoes.

Money. A lot of money.

In a slow motion, Willow eased his hand down to the man's throat and checked for a pulse. His eyes were open in death, black like a night without stars. "He's dead," Willow announced.

There was a shout from someone in the back. "Is that money?"

The group moved forward like a small wave toward the man on the ground. Fingers were pointed in his direction. There were gasps. One-by-one, the row of shocked expressions lined the interior of the pavilion as if no one knew exactly what to do.

"We have to call the police," Willow offered. He stood up and checked the size of the crowd. "This has to be reported."

Lucas Park took a step forward. "And what about all that money? The message said come get it."

Willow turned to Park. "But we didn't know the money would be on a dead man."

Park pushed his agenda. "The police are going to be here soon. I say we just take a few bills. What will it matter?" Around him, there was a smattering of voices, all in agreement.

Willow again tried to instill reasoning. "This is a police situation. We can't just take some money. We can't."

A voice from the back. "Who put you in charge?"

Park pointed to Willow. "You can't stop all of us."

"Now just stay right where you are. I'm going to call the police." One second after Willow reached for his cell phone, he was rushed by the mob. Park led the assault. Willow was pushed to the ground. He was deflecting boots and shoes. His right leg was stepped on three times. All of his energy was centered on standing up or risk being stomped to death. Hands were thrust into the shirt of the man. Seconds later, the shirt was ripped off in the frenzy. The sound of hands slapping away other hands, and voices yelling echoed through the tiny park.

The man's shoes were ripped off. There was more money in his pants. Hundred and fifty-dollar bills were snatched up quick. The throng was like a hungry gathering of sharks devouring a kill. The bills were jammed into pockets, and inside blouses. One man thrust them down the inside back of his shirt like a collection bag. Satiated and convinced there were no more hundreds to pick through, people started to back up and retreat to their cars. Willow kept a few bills, pushing them inside the top of his pants. Guilt swept over him like a summer tornado.

Sirens pierced the night air. The sound sent everyone rushing to get away. Car tires spat rocks. Smoke from all the cars leaving caused Willow to choke. He slow-walked to his car and left. When he pulled away, the figure in the pavilion was moved a few feet from the original position. All of the clothes were torn off and the man was naked.

Willow wanted to go back and put something on him. He changed his mind and drove home.

# 3

"In my years on the force, I've never seen anything like this." Detective Mark David stood twenty feet from the body in the pavilion. He was wearing booties over his shoes and gloves. By his side was detective Sam Dustin.

Dustin watched the crime scene techs move through a slow process of casting the dozens of footprints. "What a mess. Our scene will never hold up in court. Thirty people contaminated the whole thing."

"It was more like twenty people, but yep, we've got a lot of work to do." Mark David looked much larger than his one-hundred-eighty pounds. He had close-cropped hair and kept a pad tucked into the waist of his pants. "How long before we can roll him over?"

A member of the tech team motioned all ten fingers. "Ten? Okay." David nodded.

"What did the caller say?" Dustin checked his watch.

"That a bunch of people, maybe a hundred, were eating some guy in the park like zombies."

"Naw. I buy the twenty people. But we got another call from someone who said they were taking money off the guy."

"Money?"

"Yep. Tons of money."

"That explains the mess." Dustin studied the area. "Any closed circuit?"

Mark David sighed. "The cameras here broke months ago. Building owners say it was on their list to fix them but they never got around to it."

The yellow police tape enclosed two city blocks. After uniforms arrived, the park was not allowed to open in the morning. The beach near the park was shut down, including the parking lot, leaving dozens looking for a space elsewhere. A police helicopter took aerial photographs, sniffers, or police dogs, did a grid search for anything connected to the body and a team of officers checked door-to-door, asking questions.

The crime techs motioned for the two detectives to move to the body following a path laid out for them.

Mark David pulled out his notebook. "Whatcha got?"

Brandon Bowers, the tech leader, spoke through the soft mask covering his mouth. "From what we can tell, he was not killed here."

"Killed, not natural?" David asked.

Bowers pointed to the victim. "He's got two in the back. No blood. It's my guess they waited until lividity started to settle and moved him here. That makes for a very heavy load. Maybe one guy could do it."

"Any I.D?"

"Nothing. Not even a tattoo. We did an initial check on fingerprints and came up with nothing." Bowers paused. "They really did a job on him."

"They?"

"I'm not talking about who killed him. I'm talking about this crowd we keep hearing about. There are actual footprints on the body. We're taking pictures. They took all the clothes off this guy."

"Okay thanks." David stopped writing. "Are the two bullets through-and-through?"

"That's the interesting thing. I'll know more when I get him on the table, but it appears someone dug out the bullets before putting him here."

"A collector?"

Bowers shook his head, as if seeing something for the first time. "He's careful. But he also knows some medical training."

Mark David was about to walk the grounds and look for items until he was held back by Bowers.

"Oh, and there's this." Bowers pointed to a brown evidence bag. "Take a look. I didn't want to seal the bag until you saw what's inside first."

The detectives walked to the bag and looked inside. A small stack of perhaps eight hundred-dollar bills were in the bag. Four of them marked with blood.

Bowers joined them. "Thought that might catch your interest. The bills were, I'm guessing, stuck to the guy. The crowd missed them. I'll process them as soon as possible. Get'm to you."

"Thanks."

Once Bowers stepped away, David turned to Dustin. "I want every piece of surveillance video checked for a square mile. They had to arrive by car or van. I need a check of every store around here. If what I think is true, that money is like burning rocks in somebody's pocket and they're going to spend it. And when they do, I want names."

They studied the man. Dustin said, "What does he look? Maybe thirty-five years old?"

"Good guess." The body had clean arms, palms and hands, meaning he didn't fight back. There was a small scar on his right temple. "Looks like somebody in the crowd kicked him."

Dustin shook his finger at the victim. "I know this guy."

"You sure?"

"Positive. I just can't make it out. His appearance has changed. Gray around the temples, but it's him. Just who, I can't remember." He leaned in closer. "But trust me, I'll remember in a bit."

# 4

Lucas Park checked on his money six times in three hours. He arranged three rows, all neatly stacked, just to the right of a pile of clean socks in the middle drawer. The grin curled high up into his face. He turned around in a quick move when he heard the bedroom door open.

"You must have some money with all that booze you brought home." Joni Park watched him move from the chest of drawers and walk out into the living room.

"Just got lucky, that's all. Played a scratch-off and got some. I never win at those things."

"Well, did you win enough to pay the rent?"

"Already left an envelope under the door."

She looked distressed. "And you didn't get a receipt?"

"Don't worry. I'll go back down there in a bit when he wakes up. Just make us some breakfast."

"With what? You know there's nothing in the house." She opened the fridge as she spoke. "Eggs and sausage? Wow. You sure were a busy somebody last night. I didn't even hear you come in."

"Went to the store, paid the rent, filled up the car with gas. Did it all."

There was a soft clatter as she pulled out pans and a small bowl. "Maybe our luck is changing."

"Maybe."

"I did hear on the radio, they have the park shut down."

"Oh?"

"Something about a body found there. You hear anything about that?"

"Nope. Been too busy shopping. They say anything else?"

"No, just that police were being real quiet about it." She cracked five eggs, poured in milk with them and started mixing. "Seems like you can't even go to the park anymore." In the next half-hour, Lucas Park dined on sausage patties, first seared, then cooked in water to keep them soft. The eggs were fluffed up and cheese was added. The toast was medium brown. They ate like it was their first real meal in years. Full, Park rested on the couch. He had been up all night and never stopped until now.

"Maybe we can get some new drapes." She opened the French doors to the balcony. The view was the best thing about the drab apartment. There was a line of four palm trees in front of her, and a long stretch of grass, all the way to the street. When the evening light was just right, the sky would form patterns of blue-gray clouds, trimmed in red. Joni spent hours sitting at the small table and watched cars poking through slow traffic toward the ocean. When she was done gazing, Joni liked to lean on the railing. She pressed her body up against the black bars and let her upper body hover over the street, as if she could fly. The rail kept her snugly in place and did not budge. Lucas had watched her hundreds of times, going through the same routine of staring, then leaning. She once told him the air purified her. "I'd like to get a new table."

She placed a foot on the balcony.

"Stop!" Park yelled at her.

"Why? You know I love it out here."

"It's just that I want to do some work out there. It's all marked off. Give me a few days and you'll get your balcony back."

"If you insist."

He leaned back until he was in just the right position to watch television. Joni waited until he was in a heavy snore. She tapped at his foot and when he did not move, she sneaked back into the bedroom. Through the years she had learned how to look for money hidden by Lucas. With both hands she eased the drawer open like she was cracking a safe. Joni touched all around until she discovered something to the right. She found the money. She picked up the stacks and rubbed the money against her face, finally kissing the crinkled one-hundred-dollar bills. For only a second, she held the bills wondering where he got so much cash. And then her question went away, replaced by the knowledge that money was in the drawer. A wave moved through her as if a bad thought was taking over her body. She fought off the urge to take one or two bills and with a crook's expertise, she closed up the drawer without making a sound.

## 5

Cason Willow showed his girlfriend the money as soon as he reached home. He didn't take much. He paced through the apartment debating making a phone call to police or staying anonymous.

Sonia Mason called in sick from her job, made tea and listened to him rant.

"You should have seen them," he started. "They were pushing each other, fighting, taking all that money from a dead man." He walked around the room thrusting his arms in the air, showing how the money was snatched.

"And you found him like that?"

"The person who sent us the message knew what would happen. They couldn't stay away from the money. It was horrible."

She picked up the few hundred-dollar bills and examined them. "They don't look fake." She rubbed the bills, holding one up to the light.

"Far as I can tell, they're real. The question is what do I do now?"

Her face contorted, as if making a mental list of the legal challenges he could face. "They could say anything, that you had something to do with his death."

"But I didn't do anything."

"You sure he was dead."

"He was cold. Yes, he was dead."

Her questions came at him like so many darts. "Did anyone check for an identification. Or a cell phone?"

"No."

"Was he alone?"

"I don't know."

"What about his car? Did anyone look for his car?"

"No, we didn't have time. I had to get out of there."

She had one more question. "You see any surveillance cameras?"

"I don't think so."

She rubbed her forehead. "The money alone could put you in trouble. Stealing, not reporting a death, obstruction of justice. They could even say you conspired with the others to take all that money."

"I tried to stop them."

"Your word against the entire group."

He started pacing again. Both his hands were jammed into his pockets, then he rested them on his belt, sat down, then got up and went to the window.

"Come have some tea. You're a wreck. You've got a test to take."

He sat down again and sipped from the cup. "I'll wait. See what the news says. See if this thing blows over or if I have to come forward. I don't want to be the first one in the door at the police station."

"That works. You can always say you were afraid the others might come after you."

He took another sip. The tea seemed to calm him.

She sat in quiet while he sipped the brew. Sonia resembled a woman knotted up in worries. A place in the carpet was worn down where she had kicked the same spot when something bothered her. During troubling times in their relationship, she worried. He worried. Both of them carried the weight of any bad circumstances. Neither had the ability to brush things off and move on right away.

Sonia pulled up three articles on the Internet. "Says here police are trying to ID him. They are looking for any help from the public." She kept reading. "There's no mention of any money." She turned from the computer and stared at him. Hard.

"Don't look at me like that. We had mob rule. Me against everyone else."

He was not good at waiting. He headed out to take the test.

# 6

---

"I should have taken more." Pam Oakman spoke out loud to herself. She pounded her fist into a pile of clothes all tagged with a half-off marker. An hour until the shop was open and her thoughts were not on the man. She kept thinking about the stash of money.

Pam kept the money in her bra, next to her heart. Part of the amount was already spent on a new sign to go in the window. Another four one-hundred-dollar bills went to the bank. The rest with her.

She winced looking at the clock. Almost 11:00 AM and her store was still closed. Outside, people walked in the shadows to get some relief from the sun, a lack of rain left lawns with patches of brown spots. Next door, the dry cleaners kept the doors open, and used a huge fan to blow air through the rented space. Two doors down, the bakery and the coffee shop were filled with customers, all of them flashing glances at the park located in the middle of the town square.

Pam watched police walk the grounds through the large store windows. When an officer knocked on her entry door, she did not answer, staying just out of view in her office. He left a business card and was gone. Pam had a limited view of the park, yet she was able to see onlookers taking photographs of the crime scene tape that was still in place. She just stood near her front door watching the very spot where the mob took money from a dead man. Pam was part of that mob. She had never done anything like it before. In college, she joined a few of her friends, shed all their clothes and streaked the dean's office. A bold compulsive move, much like the one just hours earlier.

She walked past a framed picture and a feeling of guilt swept through her. She stopped and put her hand up to the photograph. The smiling face in the picture looked just like Pam. She reasoned her slow actions might have killed her daughter. It was her one continuing thought. Too damn slow.

Just like with the dead man and the money.

While she stayed back, Pam could have jumped to the front and scooped up as much as possible. The others did. Why not Pam? When the clock notched noon exactly, she opened the door. The next time she vowed, she would be ready. She wiped her forehead. "I'm getting hot," she said to no one in particular.

# 7

Mark David was on his third cup of coffee. Dustin was on the phone. When he put the phone down, David started briefing him. "So, we might have an ID on him. Dental records say the guy is Kulis Barney, age thirty-nine, last known address is Fort Lauderdale, after moving from Stilton Bay almost six years ago. He has no priors, and worked on cars when he was here."

"Is that coffee fresh?" Dustin reached for his cup.

"It's hot. Don't know if it's fresh."

"What does it taste like?" He poured a half-cup and gulped.

"Like fresh-squeezed shoe leather."

"Ummm. Love it." Dustin sat back down. "This guy have any relatives?"

"Not that I can find."

There was an unspoken cadence between them. A certain ritual while working a case, making sure everything was checked out. David once remarked how their pace was like a turtle on steroids, slow yet plodding until the finish line was apparent.

Sam Dustin's hand almost covered his face, as he examined a list on a pad. His size forty-two jacket was never buttoned as it was one size too small. He left the top shirt button undone and let the tie knot hang loose against a wrinkled collar. The knot was so old the thing had a layer of dust from years of merely being pulled off and thrown on a dresser top. On the tip of the tie was a dried blood stain from a case four years earlier. He never took the time to do a fresh knot. "We need another person on this?"

Mark David shrugged off the question as if he heard it for the third time. "We can handle it ourselves." A line of questions hit him. "The uniforms are outside his house waiting for us. The warrant came through a few minutes ago, but where is this guy's car? The uni's say it's not there."

Mark David wiped down his face with his hands. "I don't get it. Why would anyone put all that money out there on the vic? What's the point?"

"And all those people crawling over a dead man to get it. I know it's money but c'mon, what a way to get some cash. You have to be desperate."

David checked his computer for any late arriving emails.

Dustin unwrapped the massive hand from his face. "We're sure his house is not the original crime scene?"

"They looked in the windows. Nothing seemed out of place." An email popped into David's computer. He opened the file. "Ah, the street cam guys got no plates. We just go door to door. We hit the houses, look for locations."

"You still say we don't need any help?"

Mark David got up to leave. "I got you. That's all I need."

# 8

————

Lucas Park counted the money for a tenth time and hit the table with his fist. The count was twelve-thousand-fifty dollars. He could coast with that amount for a short period, still, it was definitely not enough for what he wanted to do.

When money was so tough for Park to generate, he wondered to himself how a person could just throw cash away, stuffed into the clothing of a corpse. For Park, greed took over practicality. Sure, he should have called the police, but how could he pass up money just resting on the ground, waiting to be claimed. The amount was far short of what he expected. Park hoped he would be the only one there.

He studied plan A again. His wife was at work, while Park was supposed to be on the hunt for a job. He waited until the complex was quiet and moved out onto the balcony with a lot of caution. Park leaned down with a screwdriver until he was hovering over the connecting bolts. Years of wind-driven rain made the bolts rusty and with some quiet nudging, Park was able to ease them free from the building. He didn't want to pull them out altogether, just enough so that with enough weight, the railing would give and topple the eight stories to the pavement below. Park also had to make sure there were no scratch marks from the screwdriver. Best he could figure, the railing was ready to fall with just a slight weight and some movement. Too many scratches would be hard to explain later.

The last bolt was moved just far enough for his satisfaction.

Perfect.

The phone rang. Park let it go to voicemail. He was one of the very few who still relied on a land-line phone. The message was another job manager turning him down. At least Joni could hear he was still actively looking and that would appease her. As he walked around the two-bedroom apartment, Park sized up the content of his life. He fixated on the house he never acquired, the good job he still did not have, the lack of money to buy anything substantial, and his share of the rent payments he met only half the year. For a man in his early fifties, Park realized the fact he was, on paper, a failure. He rubbed small circles at his temples. He conjured himself to be a taker, someone who would grab what was needed in life, no matter what his wife said.

His dreams were consumed with ways to kill her. There were desires to take her on a trip out of the country, to a remote hike near spectacular views on a cliff. A simple nudge would do. Just watch her go over the rocks. A simple explanation that she lost her balance and there was nothing he could do. Only he didn't have the money for such a trip. There were imaginary plans of leaving her in a jungle, pushing her down the stairs or even notions of hiring a hit man. Hiring someone, Park reasoned, would involve too many other people. No, his very simple plan of working on the balcony railing was still his best option. While he worked so diligently on the railing, he kept up the appearance of a dutiful, out-of-work husband.

For almost two hours, Park vacuumed the rugs, pulled and stacked the clean dishes from the machine, wiped down the countertops, and cleaned the dreaded man-messes in the bathroom. He dared staring at the balcony just a few too many times. When Joni got back from work, he wanted her to feel comfortable with the appearance he was trying to hold up his end.

# 9

Two uniforms waved at Mark David as he approached the home of Kulis Barney with a warrant in his right hand. The home was two-bedroom, one car garage, tucked under five spreading ficus trees. One good puff from a hurricane and the trees would topple onto the roof. David figured the guy was lucky the home was in one piece. Sam Dustin carried in a stash of evidence bags. Behind Dustin was a two-person crime tech team.

Once the front door was properly dusted for prints, David made his way inside. The place was immaculate. Dustin checked a few times and could not find anything under the chairs, couch or sofa. The countertops were whistle-clean and even the top of the fridge appeared dirt-free.

The techs went through the books, gloves on, picking at the pages for anything to fall out. Mark David checked the master bedroom. The bed was made and there were no signs of a woman.

"Not even a condom," Dustin said. "This guy was a hermit."

"And no money and no blood. Whatever happened to him, I don't think it happened here."

The techs sprayed for evidence of blood in just about every location in the house and garage. Throughout the search, the techs kept indicating nothing was useful.

"This guy didn't even have pictures on the wall." David looked down at the small collection of CDs. "Anyone see a wallet? Or car keys?" Quiet.

They walked from room to room, searched the garage and met back in the kitchen. David opened and closed the fridge, then turned to his partner. "Does this place look too clean?"

"Yep."

Just then, the crime techs indicated they were almost finished, with one tech saying the carpet did not appear to have any blood stains. The place was criminally clean.

They were just about to go outside and talk to neighbors when a uniform appeared at the door. "I don't want to come inside," he said.

Mark David said, "that's okay. We're coming outside."

The sun had dried off any hint of morning dew and the glare on car windows made one hold up a hand to block the rays or put on sunglasses. The officer held out a folder and handed the file to Sam Dustin. The detective thanked the officer and pulled out the paperwork. There was a look on his face as if he had just hit all the numbers of the Florida lottery. Dustin slapped the side of his leg so hard, the thump made everyone around him take notice.

Mark David approached him. "What is it?"

"It just hit me where I saw this vic before. I knew it!" A laugh started in his gut and rattled through his body until what came out of his mouth was a roar as if the contents of a vault hidden for thousands of years were just exposed only to him.

Mark David scowled. "This isn't funny."

"Can't help it." He handed the file over to David. "Didn't mean to laugh, but I've been saying this for years and no one would listen. Take a look at whose bloody prints came up on the money. You won't believe this."

# 10

One hour after the rain stopped, a single drop gathered on the gutter until finally falling on the shoulder of Queenie Erum, sliding over the small heart tattoo above her left breast and disappearing into the well-developed cleavage. She patted at the moisture like a gnat was burrowing down into her bra. "Damn rain," she said.

Across the street, inside a rusty gray van, private investigator Frank Tower checked once again to make sure he was recording video and snapping pictures through a dark-tinted portal. Tower had spent months preparing the van, putting up black curtains along the inside panels, a block-out wall behind the driver's seat, a chair mounted on rails in order to slide back and forth between his equipment and even a small bathroom in the corner, so he wouldn't have to leave. Tower pressed an eye to the lens of the video camera. He saw Erum walk around the front of the house wearing six-inch stiletto heels. "Gotcha," he said to the wall.

Queenie Erum was wearing a micro skirt and a black blouse. She kept looking up as if to check for another drop headed downward. She moved to a car fifteen feet away and stopped for a second to admire her long legs and short skirt in the reflection of the window. Then she took off. Erum was not walking, she was in a trot, part run. From inside the van, Tower smiled. She pulled a box from the car, turned to the house and yelled. "Roland, get out here. Now! It's still raining."

Roland Zuro, almost six-foot tall with cupboard stiff shoulders, big hands and no sign of a limp. Zuro walked to Erum and took the box from her, lifting the thing above his head like it was a paper cup. Tower zoomed in with his camera.

Both Erum and Zuro were in the front yard, talking loudly, then they moved inside. A few minutes later, Zuro reemerged. This time, he went to the car carrying what looked like a pool pump. Tower figured the pump had to weigh at least sixty pounds. In the van, next to the camera, a table was bolted to the metal. Tower kept a pad available and he was busy now, writing down notes on what he was observing.

Zuro tossed the pump into the trunk of the car. Confrontation was not part of Tower's mandate. He was there to simply record and report. And get paid.

Tower checked his notes. On the top sheet was a request from the client. The company listed Zuro and Erum as employees at the warehouse. During the day, they did not show themselves as being girlfriend and boyfriend. They ate lunch at separate tables and never conversed. Tower discovered they both lived at the same address, different from the one in her employee file. In his notes, he indicated sixteen days of watching the pair after they put in workers comp complaints seven months ago. Erum claimed she almost snapped her ankle on a raised portion of the warehouse floor and could not walk or do daily work requirements. Home rest, she insisted, was what the doctors told her. She was merely complying by walking with a cane and taking very short walks for therapy. Tower was eager to show Erum's injury-damaged ankle was just fine while running in six-inch heels.

Zuro's claim was for lifting heavy boxes at the warehouse. He told his bosses he couldn't stand up straight without a wall of pain developing in his lower back. He too had a doctor say he was limited to a full-paid rest. Erum's attorney sent the company a letter indicating her intention to sue over the fall, while Zuro wanted permanent disability.

Tower had gathered days of video showing the pair moved a dead tree, jacked up a car, hauled in bags of new mulch and once Zuro picked her up over his shoulders and tossed her, where she landed with the grace of an Olympic gymnast, worthy of a perfect score. Three days earlier, he followed them to Miami where he used a button camera to get video of them dancing well past 2:00 A.M.

Tower thought it was impressive how they waited several months, then started operating out in the public, flaunting their fraud with impunity, parading with a certain level of audacity.

Tower decided his part of the case was over. He had plenty of video and now had to prepare a long report. His last memory of a full night's sleep was more than a month ago. He drove the banged-up van back to his office near downtown Stilton Bay. He kept the van in a garage, far from prying eyes. The outside was a mixture of bondo gray paint and faded blue streaks. Two wheels did not match and the right rear was bald. The thing blended right into the street.

When he pulled up, he saw two familiar faces. Mark David got out of the car first, followed by Sam Dustin. They looked serious.

"What's up boys?" Tower said, stretching and yawning.

"Been working hard?" Mark David looked past Tower at the van.

"Yep. But I'm done." Tower watched Dustin move a bit to his right. "Something wrong? Sammy here is flanking me."

"We've known each other a long time." Mark David kept his tone even.

"Yeah." Tower sounded curious. "Especially when you count those five years we were partners on the force."

David moved in closer. "We have to talk. Down at the station."

"Talk? About what?"

"Where were you last night?" The question came from Dustin, who was directly on Tower's right side.

"Working. Spent the last three nights on a stake-out. I'm really tired. What is this about?"

"Not here," David said. "You know this routine better than anyone. I trust you with my life Frank, but we need to talk and we have to do it now."

"You mind telling me what's up? I haven't seen a newspaper or the news in days."

Dustin put his hand on his weapon. "Just come down with us, quiet and we'll just take it from there."

# 11

Tower appealed to Mark David. "We've been through too much. Just lay it out for me."

David looked uncomfortable. "We have to pursue this. I just have to be sure of where you've been in the last few days."

Tower pointed to the banged-up van. "You see that piece of junk? I've been living in that thing for three days. Eat, piss and sleep in that van. Been working a case, and no, I can't talk about it, but I assure you I've been right there."

Dustin threw a question. "Anyone else can vouch for that?"

"No. I work alone most of the time. Look, all my video is time-stamped. You can check the neighbors and pull any surveillance camera video you want, I called a couple of times, so you can tri-angulate my location. Check the van, check anything. I have nothing to hide."

Mark David pulled out his note pad and looked into the eyes of his former partner. "We found a body. Male, shot twice. If it's okay with you, we'd like to see your weapon."

"You're sayn' I shot a male vic? Twice?" Rage was boiling up in Tower's voice.

"You haven't heard the best parts." Dustin looked Tower up and down as though looking to see if he was armed.

"First of all, both of you know me. Frank Tower, five years on the force. You know I wouldn't be mixed up in something like you're describing."

Dustin tossed another question. "Then, how is it we found your prints on some money found on the victim?"

"I don't know. That could have been a contact with this person months ago."

Dustin continued. "Your prints were found in some blood."

Tower's face could not hide the flush of thoughts going on in his head. Stacking and re-stacking his last few days. "I can honestly say I have not been anywhere except in this van and a couple of times to my office. Haven't even been home." Tower had a few questions of his own. "Where was he found?"

David answered. "The pavilion at the park. Downtown."

"And you have an ID on this guy?"

Dustin cut in to make sure he delivered the information. "His name is Kulis Barney. That name mean anything to you?"

Tower thought about the question. "It does sound familiar?"

A smile ripped across Dustin's face. "That's the best part. It's the guy who said you stole money at a crime scene. Money that was taken then or later from the evidence room."

"I was cleared of that. You know that."

"That was then," Dustin said. "This is now. He implicated you. Now, that guy is dead. He has your prints on him."

Tower recalled some old facts. There was a long, involved fraud investigation, resulting in a raid on a business and the collection of money from seventy to eighty-thousand dollars. Mark David and Tower were assigned to guarding the money before transport to the evidence room. David was called off to another scene, leaving just Tower and the money. Only the money never arrived. Tower saw the money being loaded onto a van and signed the paperwork as the witnessing officer. When the box made it to the evidence room, it was empty. The two city employees in the van passed lie detector tests, as did Tower. Where did the money go? Kulis Barney stepped forward to say he thought he saw Tower do something with a box. Not much for investigators, but it was enough to get Tower suspended. An investigation cleared him and the money was never found. Tower only recalled he heard a commotion near his location and briefly looked outside. Just seconds. Long enough for someone to switch the boxes. Once he was cleared, a few years later, Tower left the force. As Dustin said, that was then. This was now.

The sky had a low ceiling of bulging clouds, all gray and ready to heave rain on anyone below, save for a small circle of sunlight, letting a ray beam down and light up the area where the men were talking. Tower spoke as if he headed the investigation himself. "You've got what? There are cameras all around the city. You can track my movements, check for my license plate. You should know I was right here."

"There's a problem with that." Mark David countered. "We had a power glitch. The cameras were down for almost three hours. Not going to lie to you. We're going through store surveillance video right now."

Dustin began moving his hands in big sweeping motions. "Your legs ain't broke! You could have left the camera running, giving you an alibi, then sneak out of the van, get into another car, pop ole Kulis with a couple of bullet kisses to the back for old-times-sake, then make it back here like nothing's wrong."

"I've been right here. No place else." Tower stood erect. His tone changed to an even delivery. "You guys are searching. And you don't have anything. I never touched this guy. You might remember he failed a lie-detector test. No one else saw what he claimed. I passed the same test. Every inch of my movements that day were verified by either other officers or video. Your hunting expedition is over. I'm done."

He reached into his bag and pulled out his Glock. "Here. Check it out. You'll see it has not been fired. I'm not working with a back-up piece. There are all kinds of ways those prints could end up there. Do your homework gentlemen! And stop pestering me. Don't you see I'm being set up?" He started for his office. "Mark, when you're done with my piece, please return it. Until then, I'll think about getting a lawyer."

## 12
---

Once inside his office, Tower watched the two detectives drive off. He immediately went to the computer and started an Internet search. He pulled up articles on the murder investigation, the free-money grab on a dead man and interviews from store owners. Tower was up-to-speed. For the next two hours, he wrote out the report on his surveillance and by computer, sent the entire package, including video to the client. The response was an overwhelming thank you as Tower was saving the company thousands of dollars, future lawyer's fees and probably stopped a lawsuit.

His attention was now on himself.

He peeled off his clothes and entered the shower. His office was equipped with most of the essentials from his home. Right now, Tower did not want to go there, opting to stay at his office where he could work his computers. He took a shower. The water was warm and soothing enough to ward off the aching in his body and eyes from a lack of sleep. Droplets cascading over him. He washed away the funk of living in a van.

Tower let each word spoken to him by the detectives go through his mind. He had a lot of questions, yet he knew the detectives wouldn't be much help. Tower easily concluded he was on a short list of suspects. When he was done drying off, he put on fresh clothes and sat down at his desk. Tower reached down and pulled back a section of the carpet, revealing a floor safe. He opened the small vault and pulled out a log book. Safe closed, he opened the book and started flipping through pages.

The log book listed all of his work history going to when he first started his agency. He ran his finger down the log and looked for anything that would bring him in-line with the victim. Kulis Barney, he remembered, at times, worked part-time at a car repair shop. Tower's second weapon, a Sig Sauer, was in the safe. Tower picked up the gun, held the piece for a few seconds, then put the gun back. Back on the computer, he discovered the repair shop was still there, under a new owner. He wrote down the address and continued his Internet search. Tower brought up and jotted down a list of businesses near the park. He also found the new location where Barney had moved.

He picked up his cell phone with the intention of calling his wife, Shannon. She was out of town on a seminar connected to her job and was not expected back for a week. Why bother her, he thought, until he had more facts. Tower locked up the safe and picked up the keys to his other car, a black BMW. His first stop would be the repair shop.

## 13

Pam Oakman wiped down the sweat off her brow for the fifth time. She ignored checking her temperature and kept the shop open. Plenty of customers were in during the day, most of them talking about the rumors of found money and the man. She pretended she didn't know anything and sold more items than she had in the past. Her best day in years.

The first cough started late in the afternoon. Oakman's eyes were a runny mess and she was starting to have a hard time focusing. By 5:00 P.M., she closed up and didn't have the strength to count the proceeds. She looked out the window and saw police were still walking through the park, looking for anything dropped or left behind. The yellow crime tape was still fluttering in the seaside breeze. Earlier, she saw a crime tech on a rooftop taking photographs of the scene. When police came, she lied about her involvement, saying she spent the night at home. Another two days, they promised, and the park would reopen.

Customers looking for a bargain always left a mess. Half-off merchandise was mixed in with the top-of-the-line wear. A pair of normally expensive headphones were near the door. She felt someone was angling to walk out with them and changed their mind.

When she turned to restack a pile of pants, she fell. Oakman looked toward the front door thinking maybe someone saw her fall.

Another hard cough. She covered her mouth and when she drew back her hand, the palm was covered in blood. The money taken from the body was strewn on the floor. She would give anything to be able to stand up, yet the floor was her only option. Another cough. This time, the red spittle spewed out of her like vomit. Oakman had to get to her cell phone. The cell phone was on the counter, next to the cash register. The thing might as well be a mile away. She tried moving her legs and got no response. Next came a yell. The first few attempts were strong. The third scream was much weaker and the cough made her eyes shut tight from the pain in her chest. Now all she could do was whisper. She looked down and her blouse was covered in blood spatter from trying to yell.

She turned on her back and saw the picture of her daughter. Something was moving through her body like an alien invasion of attack germs. Oakman was sure her body temp was rising. Her chest felt as though warm hands were pressing down on her lungs, squeezing and massaging them, letting out just a tiny bit of air, letting the alien body take over. There was a moment there, where she was sleeping. She jolted for just an instant as she realized the feeling was not sleep.

Death had arrived.

Pam Oakman was drifting between two worlds. When her eyes were open, she knew where she was and generally what was happening. On her back, she saw the afternoon sun track columns of light across the ceiling. Then, she would close her eyes and drift into the other world of shadows and quiet. Slipping between life and death. She used up the last of her energy to concentrate on her daughter. Guilt washed through her. Oakman focused on the memories of her daughter and what she could have done. Maybe if she had acted right away, her daughter would still be alive. Why did she hesitate to take more money off the body? When she felt the first symptoms, why didn't she call her doctor? Again, and again, she had hesitated. The thought stayed with her since it happened, how hesitation killed her daughter and now she was going to die. Pam Oakman's breathing was shallow, barely enough to puff up the chest of a bird. Her fingers flattened out and she let her body go limp. Slipping again, in and out, soft breaths, and no more fighting.

Her eyes stayed closed much longer than she was awake. The vise-like feeling in her chest was taking the last of her breath and she didn't have the power to produce a wheeze. The air was ebbing out of her body and she let death move through her like a warm blanket being pulled up to her neck, a feeling of warm serenity too strong to resist. And then she was gone.

# 14

"Leave now, or I call the police." Jed Moonstellar was covered in car grease from his steel-toed work boots to the broken glasses held together with tape.

Frank Tower held his ground. "I just want to ask a couple of questions and I'll be out of here, I promise." Tower waited for a reaction. Moonstellar had no customers in the shop. A faded blue Toyota was up on the lift.

"I'm short today," Moonstellar looked at the small office. "My office clerk called in sick."

"Tell you what, if anyone shows up, I'll leave. I don't want you to lose any customers. Just a couple of questions."

"A couple." Moonstellar pushed the damaged glasses back up on his nose. The place smelled of burnt oil and transmission fluid. On a back wall was a row of dirty rags just below a calendar. Tower noticed the month was not current. The front office had clean black and white tiles with a dirty plastic bubble on a stand, full of gum for children.

"Why did Kulis Barney come back? He's been gone for years."

Moonstellar moved about like he didn't want to answer. Tower tried another question. "When did he come back?"

"Two weeks ago."

"Was he staying with you?"

"Yes."

Tower tried again. "And, why did he come back?"

"Someone called him. He said some big deal was in the works."

"He say what the deal was about?"

Moonstellar stepped on a roach. "Wouldn't tell me. Big secret."

"This person who called him, do you know him?"

"He never mentioned a name." Moonstellar almost dropped the wrench in his hands. "You know the police asked me some of the same questions."

"Did they check out the room you let him use?"

"Yeah, but I don't think they found anything."

Moonstellar looked up at the clock. 10:34 A.M. "Look, I'm talking to you because you've always been good for my business, bringing your cars here. And your mother helped my sister."

"You mean Jackie. I don't refer to her as my mom."

"Yeah, Jackie. Helped my sis get off the drugs. Thanks."

"Any chance I can see that room?"

"Sure, but not until I get off work. Say about six?"

"That will work."

Tower thanked him and got into his car. He drove to the park and watched two uniforms sitting in their cars guarding the crime scene. He moved past them and found a parking spot. Once out of his car, Tower didn't have a clear plan in mind. He thought he would ask a few business owners if they saw anything. He only had the articles for information. He noticed a few people tried to enter a consignment shop, only to find a locked door. Tower approached.

"Are they usually open by now?" Tower asked a woman.

"Yes, but not today." She walked away.

Tower cupped his hands, pressing against the glass and looked into the store. He saw piles of clothing in small and large stacks, neat and cluttered. There was no movement inside. He was just about to leave when he saw something. He pulled out his phone and called 9-1-1.

"Hello. Get fire rescue here now. I see what looks like a woman passed out on the floor. Yes. Get here now." A person to Tower's right said the back door was also locked. Fire rescue would take two to three minutes to arrive. Tower took a step back and drove his shoulder into the doorframe. On the second try, the door smashed open. Tower ran to the person on the floor. He saw her color was off and he reached for a pulse. Two people walked in behind Tower. He looked around for anyone else in the store and saw no one there. He drew his hand back.

When the fire rescue truck arrived, two others came with them. Detective Mark David and his partner.

# 15

"She's dead, Mark." There was a certain resignation in Frank Tower's voice, a gave-it-all-I-could low key timbre, coming from a worn-down PI.

"Frank, what are you doing here?" Mark David looked like a man who didn't know what to do with his hands. He raised up his right hand, then lowered it. The movement looked like a guy about to put his arm around an old friend. Tower knew he wasn't an old buddy right now. He was a murder suspect in a case where the main person just showed up at the scene where there was a body.

"The temp is off," Tower said. "And the coloring is wrong."

"Coloring?" David asked.

"Take a close look at her skin, her eyes. Something is going on. The medical examiner can tell you. If I had to guess, I'd say she was poisoned."

"Are you confessing?" Sam Dustin stood with his right hand on his weapon.

Tower looked back at the person on the floor. "She's been dead for a long time. Rigor is set. To me, that puts her death at just about the time I was talking to the both of you."

Mark David looked over Tower. "You really need to get some sleep. But before that, please tell me what you were doing here? And don't say shopping."

"I can't lie to you. You'd know. I wanted to see the park scene. From a distance." Tower threw up his hands to back up his words.

"You know you can't do that." David looked like a teacher about to send someone to detention. "And what? You just happened to find her?"

Dustin studied Tower. "Why did you bust in here, when two officers were just down the street? You didn't think to call them?"

"Old habits." Tower returned the glare. "My instincts kicked in and I saw her, I got inside."

Dustin kept pressing. "But even then, you still didn't call in our officers."

"I called 9-1-1. She was dead and I wasn't going to leave her."

Dustin stepped closer to Tower's face. "I still don't get why you're here."

"I can go anywhere I want. Mark and I used to patrol this block for years. I know everyone here. In fact, I know her. That's Pam Oakman."

"I remember." Dustin slapped the side of his pants.

Tower said, "You might remember, the newspaper was all over the story. Pam's daughter died from an intestinal blockage. Pam ignored her daughter's plea of stomach pain and never took her to the hospital. When the pain was too much, the daughter called 9-1-1 herself. She died an hour later. Pam blamed herself. But the doctor said she would have died anyway."

Mark David finished the story. "But Pam still blamed herself. Thought she moved too slow to do anything."

"Suicide?" Sam Dustin watched another crime tech enter the building.

"I don't think so," Tower spoke so the growing crowd could not hear him. "I think there's something else going on. There's scratch marks on the floor. Things are knocked over, like this took her by surprise. If this was a suicide, it would be somewhere personal, like at home, or in a bathtub. No, I think someone got to her."

# 16

Frank Tower was told to wait outside. The detectives were inside the shop. He watched the crime techs bringing out evidence bags, more crime tape put up, and traffic inching to a near-stop as drivers angled in their seats to get a glimpse of the activity. Twenty-seven minutes later, Mark David approached Tower.

"Are you still going with suicide?" Tower was leaning against his car.

"You know I can't get into that." He was still wearing gloves and was in the process of pulling them off. "I can't have you doing your own investigation."

"If you think I'm going to sit back and let Sam Dustin figure out my future, you're wrong. I don't trust him. Not now, not ever."

David shoved the gloves down into his pocket. "Here's the deal. We've still got a lot of questions for you."

Tower stood up straight. "You know me, Mark. You know I couldn't be a part of this. I never met Kulis Barney even when the trouble with the money happened. I'm not a part of what happened to Pam Oakman. I was in a van. You can see the video I shot. You're wasting my time and yours."

"Frank, we have to be sure."

"Sure?" Tower lowered his voice. "We were partners on these streets for years. I had your six. You were the best man at my wedding. You can see I'm being set up here."

"Once we get all the facts and line them up, we can eliminate you."

Tower looked over David's shoulder. Dustin was out of the building and on the phone. "I'm sorry, but I can't just sit still and do nothing. I won't get in the way of your investigation. I promise."

"It has to be more than a promise. You have to stay out of the way right now."

"I saw the money on the floor." Tower paused to see if he would get a reaction from Mark David.

"What about it?"

Tower said, "I read about people finding money on the body. Was Pam there? Did she get some of that money?"

"Again, I can't share any of that."

"We've shared a lot. Even though I'm not on the force anymore."

"Not this time. You're too close to this. You're directly involved."

Behind them, a uniform was taking down the crime tape. Traffic moved a bit faster. Pam Oakman's body was removed, and gawkers started to walk away. Normal was coming back to the street. A build-up of clouds, a small dip in the temperature and a brisk wind all gave hint to rain coming in the next few minutes. Florida's way of warning everyone Mother Nature was coming.

A view down the block brought memories of when he was in uniform with Mark David. Two blocks away years earlier, Tower had smashed the window of a car where an infant was asleep in his child seat. The inside temp of the car had to be one-hundred-twenty degrees. The child was unharmed thanks to Tower, and the mother was charged with neglect. Three blocks away, Tower and David broke up a theft ring, breaking down a door and using an informant's tip to find the location of a fencing operation. More than a hundred-thousand in merchandise was recovered. They both received commendations for their efforts and were named officers of the month. Their work was a clean sheet of proud take-downs until the day the money went missing. Everything changed after that, with Tower resigning and David accepted into the ranks of detective.

Dustin was now standing next to Tower. "You explain yourself? What you were doing here?"

Mark David readjusted the sunglasses on his face. "You do anything else as part of your own investigation? Something we should know about?"

Tower shook his head. "I'd appreciate it if you could clear me."

Dustin put his hands on his hip in the area where he kept his handcuffs. "We need you to either come with us, or we can do this the old-school way."

"You don't need cuffs for me. I want to find out what I can, just like you."

Dustin pulled his hand from his belt. "Good. Cause we've got a warrant here to search your house, your cars, and your office."

## 17

Sam Dustin kept Frank Tower's car in front of him as they followed him to the office location, just west of downtown Stilton Bay. A line of clouds stretched across the horizon, puffed up and for the moment, blocked the blunt force of the midday sun.

Mark David was quiet most of the way, going over notes. "You went over the videotapes in Oakman's place?"

"Everything she had." Dustin's eyes never strayed from the back of Tower's car. "The night of the money grab off the body, her own interior surveillance cameras were working and got her coming back in at 1:36 AM. It was clear she was holding what looks like money. The inside cameras then confirmed it. Small stacks of one-hundred-dollar bills."

"Anything show what she did with them?"

"Some of it she stuffed down her bra. Other bills went to her purse. When we checked the purse, there were no bills."

David was writing something down. "Okay. And this morning?"

"There is video of her throughout the day, with customers. She doesn't look right. Something was going on with her."

"If it was suicide, she wouldn't be working like that all day. Doesn't make sense."

"Exactly." Dustin turned a corner. "You can see by the cameras, that she was not expecting to go down. Something put her down. She tries to get up but can't."

David stopped writing. "You see anyone in the vid who could be our perp?"

"Yeah, I thought about that. Not really. Lots of moms and general customers. I didn't even see her take a drink. Not sure how her death occurred."

"Medical examiner promised something by this afternoon."

They watched Tower pull into the driveway of his office and get out. The place was a house converted into three rooms of office space and a conference room. The entire block was a line of houses turned into law offices, real estate, a travel agency and two tax preparation businesses. "We forced the palm reader out two years ago." Tower's attempt at humor was met with stone faces.

Dustin came up to Tower, hand out. "Okay, you know the drill. Give me the keys. You wait out here."

Tower tossed the ring at him. "I can stay in the back of the room. I promise, I won't interfere."

Dustin nodded. They all went inside. When Tower had the extra money, he hired an office clerk. Today, the desk in the small entry room was vacant. Off to the right was Tower's office. The detectives started there, snapping on gloves and looking around the space. They took out books, lifted everything off the floor, checked the bathroom, pulled out every drawer, and even looked behind the curtains.

"Can I see the warrant," Tower asked.

While the two men searched, Tower read.

"Where's your client books?" Dustin's voice showed signs of weariness, like he needed to hit the gym.

"Your warrant doesn't say anything about my private books. And if that's what you want, we're headed to court."

David gave a look like he wanted to move on. "You have any other weapons here?"

Tower opened up the closet and pulled out a shotgun, a second Glock and all the ammunition. "You can check all of them."

Tower was confident they wouldn't find anything, and the client books were down under the desk in the floor safe. There was no mention of the safe in the warrant. More than thirty minutes later, they moved to the other rooms. Tower heard the rumblings coming from Dustin's stomach. Working into the afternoon without lunch will make that happen.

The detectives looked around the rooms as if they were doing a mental check on anything they might have missed. "We're headed to your house next. You want to come?" David started pulling off the gloves.

"Sure."

"I hope you don't mind riding with us," Dustin started. "The crime techs will be here in three minutes to check the van and the car. You have a choice. Stay here and watch them or come with us to the house."

"I'll go to the house."

Tower gave over his car keys and got into the back of the unmarked. An immediate feeling of claustrophobia set in. The door would not open from the inside. The seats were there for the arrested, the disdained of society, murderers, ID thieves, bank robbers and anyone questioned by the investigation side of the Stilton Bay police department. And now, Tower.

He leaned back in the seat and watched the scenery go by. Tower decided to do the same thing as the detectives. Go through a check-list of items for or against his possible arrest. Tower reasoned the only thing they had on him was the fingerprint. The case against him, he figured, was circumstantial at best. If they had other prints, he would have been confronted with them by now. There were no witnesses, no videotape, no possible link to a man found dead in the park, packed down with money. Tower sat up in the seat. There was one other thing. The victim was a witness to the alleged theft of evidence money. Tower knew he was lying since he had nothing to do with the theft. The lie-detector backed up Tower. Another weak link. Tower again leaned back in the seat.

All three men spent almost ninety minutes in the house. They were carefully going through anything belonging to Tower's wife, Shannon. He would explain the mess later. She wasn't due home for another few days. Dustin came out of the house looking frustrated. Tower stood off to the side as patient as a sniper under cover.

"We're done," David said. "We'll drop you back at your office." He tossed the keys at Tower.

When they reached Tower's office, the crime techs were just finishing up. He wanted them talking. The whole group of them, all shaking their heads like the trip was worthless. Tower checked the crime tech van and counted more than eleven evidence bags. In Tower's mind, they collected fibers from the trunk and floorboards, dusted everywhere, took photographs, swabbed and picked at lint.

"You want to give it a wash?" Tower yelled to them.

"Your car doesn't need a wash. It needs a paint job." Dustin got into the unmarked.

Mark David stepped up to Tower. "I know you didn't do this."

"Then why are you rattling my cage? You two are wasting time. The real person for this is out there, somewhere, laughing."

"Just don't do anything stupid. I know you. Give us a couple of days, and we'll remove you from the list."

"Two days, huh?" Tower's words were dripping with sarcasm.

"You know what I mean. We'll get it done soon. Just don't get in the way."

Tower watched the unmarked car pull out and drive down the block, followed by the team of crime techs. Once they were gone, Tower checked his watch. He still had time to go by the car mechanic's house and check Kulis Barney's room.

# 18

Jed Moonstellar kept checking his watch. "This won't take long, will it? I have to pick up my girlfriend."

Tower was snapping on gloves, following close behind Moonstellar. "Nope. Just a couple of minutes."

He led Tower to the back of the house, through a narrow hallway with walls of faded green paint. As he opened the door to the room, Moonstellar's glasses fell off his face and he caught them in mid-air before they clattered to the wood floor. The room was a standard ten-by-twelve, a window off to the right and a small closet. The twin bed was pushed into the corner and a small end table gave the place a dorm look.

"No phone in here?" Tower talked over his shoulder, moving toward the closet.

"No phone. Just a room." Again, Moonstellar looked at his watch.

"And you say the police have already been here?"

"Yes." The glasses got another shove.

"You need some new glasses," Tower said.

The closet was almost empty except for a piece of clothing seldom used in south Florida, a sweater. Tower walked and looked about the room, turning over the twin bed, checking the drawers, even looking under the lamp.

"Done?" There was a tone of impatience in Moonstellar's voice.

"Almost." Tower sat on the bed. He looked around the room with the stare of an eagle looking for a sign. He noticed the baseboard. "You do any work recently in here?"

"Naw. But I need to do something in this room."

Tower walked over to the baseboard and gave a section of wood a gentle pull. The piece snapped off in one quick crack. "Okay, I think we got something."

Both men stared down and saw a small depression in the base of the wall. Before Tower did anything, he pulled out his phone and snapped a few pictures. "I can't touch this, but this is your house Jed. Can I suggest something?"

Moonstellar leaned down toward the floor. "Yeah, what?"

"To cover both our asses, call detective Mark David and let him know. Obviously, the police did not find this, right?"

"Correct."

Tower gave him directions. "Okay, then I would say don't touch it, but call them, is that clear?"

"Yes."

Tower got down on the floor. There were two objects. One was a thumbdrive stuck neatly in a crevice. And there was a tiny piece of paper with numbers. Tower took several pictures and stood up. "Please tell them I did not touch anything except pull off the baseboard. They can do the rest. Okay?"

"Got it."

"Thanks for letting me in."

Tower waited until he reached his house before studying the photographs. Leaning against a pile of couch cushions, Tower expanded the cell picture. The piece of paper had four things listed. Each line was a set of numbers. He thought about what he was seeing. They were not random numbers, and instead, they were dates. Each was a set of exact dates, with the years. The first date listed looked familiar, yet Tower wasn't quite sure of its meaning. He googled each date and got all sorts of responses and not the ones he was seeking. The dates just didn't make sense.

Tower left a voicemail message for Shannon, knowing she was at some fancy dinner as her conference was drawing to a close. He poured a glass of white wine, streamed Nat King Cole through the sound system and kept thinking about the four dates. And there was the thumbdrive. He fought off the powerful urge to look for a computer at Moonstellar's house and decided an obstruction of justice charge would not be a good thing. Leave it to Mark David and pull out a finding later. He kicked up the volume and let the music fill up the house.

The lack of sleep over a four-day period was overpowering Tower. He wrestled in the folds of the couch, moving facts around and trying to weigh who would put his fingerprints at a death scene. Shannon seeped into his thoughts like warm fingers massaging his head. The first time he met her was on the beach at Stilton Bay, just finishing a run and seeing Shannon chasing after her hat blowing away from her in the playful Atlantic air. He managed to catch up to the straw hat and in giving it back to her, focused on her eyes and stayed hooked throughout the wedding three months later. Tower's eyes closed to a fanciful dream with the both of them. He was in a good place and not aware of any possible tormentor in the darkness. The depths of his sleep took Tower to places far reaching into his mind and not on the vast world just outside his door.

# 19

"You're late." Medical examiner Elly Kent was tapping her right foot, when detective Mark David and his partner entered the realm of the morgue. David felt the phone rattle in his pocket and ignored the call. Before him was the body of Kulis Barney. "Sorry. And you say this is urgent?"

"I got you in here right away, 'cause this is not good." She rubbed her brow with her forearm. "I know you like to be here for the start of these, but I couldn't wait. And what I'm seeing needed to get to you as soon as possible."

"Explain."

"The problem is not with Kulis." She pointed to another room. A body was inside a sealed vault with a lock on the door. The detectives looked through a large viewing window. "The concern is with her."

"Pam Oakman?" David was confused.

Kent rolled the body closer to the detectives. "We are still working up the toxicology, which will take some time, but we got some preliminary results." Her hair was pulled back, making her forehead look larger than normal. The brown eyes showed the confidence she earned from years of examining victims. When she spoke, no one questioned her opinion.

Both men stepped closer to the window. Kent was nervous, more nervous than at any autopsy David could remember. "You got my attention."

"We have verified she died from poison. Just which one is still under investigation. But here's why we called you in." Kent paused, as if thinking about what she was about to say. "My staff and I agree, Pam Oakman has all the signs that she was poisoned from the money."

"The money?" David realized he was shouting and lowered his voice. "You mean the money found at the scene?"

"Correct. The same money taken off the body of Kulis Barney. This woman died from a touch-poison, just days after she grabbed up that cash."

Mark David and his partner stood, letting the information move through them. "Shit," he said, reaching for his note pad. "If she was poisoned, a lot of people touched that money. And we have reason to think she gave money to others, like the bank."

Kent let out a sigh. "Now, you see what I mean. There is no other explanation. Pam Oakman and many others handled poisoned money. And right now, that money is being shared all over Stilton Bay." Kent jammed her hands into her doctor's lab coat. "We put her in a quarantined area because we don't quite know what we're dealing with. A few of her organs just broke down like someone victimized by ricin."

"Oh shit," Dustin spoke to the glass in front of him.

"We have not had any other cases?" David was writing down notes.

Kent shrugged. "So far, no. But you have to get the word out. This stuff could be dangerous, whatever it is."

"What happened to her, exactly?" Dustin turned to Kent.

"Well, first, this is not ricin. Tests showed as much. But we have not been able to pinpoint the poison." She let out a deep breath. "Well, from what we believe, in her case, first she would feel her breathing tighten. From what we can determine, you might hear a wheezing sound, then later, she would have been struggling for air." Kent stared down at Oakman. Her body was cut open with the usual Y-pattern done by any coroner. "Just look at her and specifically, look at the lungs. Basically, without getting into all the technical terms, her lungs just filled with blood. She drowned in her own blood."

"How do you tell the public the money in their hands might kill them?" David was done writing.

"One other thing." Kent grabbed up an evidence bag, filled with money. "Not all of the bills tested positive. Some of this stuff is just old money."

David said, "What about the money found on Barney's body?"

"Same thing. Some of it tested positive for poisoning. The rest did not."

"Thanks." David was almost out the door.

A woman entered the room. She was around five-foot-ten, with black hair, and a welcoming smile. She started to turn around and leave.

Kent stopped her. "Don't go. This is my assistant, Vera Rossin. She's been with me for the past seven months, moved over from the West Coast."

Both men nodded a hello. Kent whispered something to Rossin, who put on a lab coat of her own. "The report you asked for is complete," Rossin said.

Kent smiled. "Thank you."

The detectives made quick steps to exit. Just as they were about to leave, a voice made Mark David stop. It was Kent. "Sorry. I have to cancel for the weekend. This is going to keep me..."

"Busy, I know." David stared at her. "We'll catch up."

In the car, Dustin was losing patience. "If Tower was involved in this..."

"I don't think it's Tower. Look at his life. He's not a killer, no matter what you think about him. Just don't know why he would be involved in all this. Poisons? That's not Tower."

"What's first?"

"Back to the office and get organized. We have to find all the money pulled off Barney and get it off the street. Now." Mark David kept ignoring the phone calls from Moonstellar. When he reached the station, the calls were an irritant he just avoided.

# 20

Joni Park coughed so hard, when she drew back her hand, blood covered her palm. She sat down and made an effort to speak. "I think I need to see the doctor."

Lucas Park seemed intrigued with her condition. He was able on three attempts to convince her to stay off the patio. All that work, he thought, loosening the bolts, yet he had to wait for the right moment. He hated helping her and fought off the urge to apply a pillow to her face in the night. Yet, if he did that, how could he collect on the four-million-dollar insurance policy? It had to be an accident. The possibilities ran through him like good ideas on a greased pad. If she fell through the railing, he could also sue the building. All this made him smile as he handed her a tissue. "You okay?"

"I don't know. I'm having a hard time breathing." She reached for her cell phone. "I'm calling the doctor. Can you drive me?"

The vision of saving her almost caused him to retch. "If you want."

"It's not like you have a job to go-," another hard cough cut off her last words. The tissue was red.

He looked at her situation and knew this could be exploited. "Maybe, you should just stay here and rest. Why go outside?"

She considered his words and kept dialing. "Hello?"

Park ventured into the bedroom and looked at the drawer containing the money. He left the cash alone since the night he gathered the bills. There was still time to wait and see if police were looking for any of the money. When he returned to the living room, Joni was on the floor. A small pool of bloody spittle was near her mouth and the cell phone was near her hand, a voice still on the other line, demanding to know if she was okay. He couldn't just leave her. There was a witness. Police might question him as standing by and doing nothing. Rather than wait for 9-1-1 to respond, he drove her to the emergency room.

When Park carried his wife into the waiting room, two nurses ran to him, asking a bevy of questions. Did she fall? When did this happen? Was she in a car crash? Were there any warning signs before she passed out? He tried to answer what he could, while filling out the paperwork. Anxious faces of the twenty people in the room stared at Joni like they were helpless and useless, all at the same time.

He was instructed to wait, and a doctor would be out to see him soon. Park studied his surroundings. Stilton Bay Medical was new to him. There were giant paintings on the wall dedicated to donors for hospital construction. The floors were clean white tile and the entire place was bathed in light.

Twenty minutes into his wait, a nurse emerged from the heavy doors and she was not accompanied by a doctor. Two large men were with her. She pointed out Park, then walked back into the bowels of the hospital. Park wanted to run and instead waited for them to approach.

"Hello, my name is detective Mark David. This is my partner Sam. We're all hoping for the best for your wife."

"Thank you." The words sounded weak.

"If we could just have a moment. Could we step over here?" Mark David took Park to an area away from prying eyes and ears. "I have to ask you first. Have you picked up any money in the past couple of days?"

# 21

Lucas Park looked as if he was thinking of what to say. "Money? No. I'm not sure what you mean."

Mark David looked around before answering. "Up to twenty people took some money off a dead man at Stilton Bay Park. Were you part of that group?"

"Me? No."

"What about your wife? Did she mention anything like that?"

"Joni? No, not to me. I'd remember something like that. Did she say that?"

David stood there studying Park. "The doctors will be out in a moment. I'm speaking to you because this is a murder investigation."

"Murder?"

"We're trying to keep this between us for the moment, but a lot of the money found on our victim contains poison. Did you, or your wife come in contact with that money? Because if you did, that would explain what they're seeing in the emergency room. That's why they called us."

"I didn't take any money. But you know, my wife went out late a couple of nights back. Thought she was making a late run to the store. I thought I saw her counting some money in the bedroom."

Dustin cut in. "Sir, if you don't mind, we're going to have to examine that money. See if it's part of the other stash. This is critical because if you touched that money, your health could be in jeopardy."

"You think my wife," Lucas put his hand up to his mouth to stifle a fake moment of emotion. "You think my wife could die?"

Mark David cautioned him. "We've already had one death. Your wife seems to be suffering from the same thing."

Park turned away from them, head bent forward. He made sure they could not see the smile breaking across his face. When he felt composed, Park turned around. "I want them to do everything they can to help her."

Dustin looked at his watch. "Your wife is sedated right now. I hate to ask you to leave here, but time is crucial for us. Can we go with Mark to check your place? I promise we'll do this as fast as possible."

"Sure. Anything to help."

The three of them walked the corridor toward the exit. The detectives let Lucas Park walk a few paces in front of them. Sam whispered to Mark David. "You believe him?"

"No. But right now we need his cooperation." He tapped his watch. "The boss has called for a meeting in one hour. I want to be able to tell him something."


Park led them inside the apartment. The two detectives fanned out across the room, eyes bouncing from one side of the place to the other, while snapping on gloves. "Where did you find her?" Dustin spoke at the wall but his comments were meant for Park.

"Right here, sir."

David was looking around as he posed questions. "Where did you see her with the money?"

"In the bedroom, at her dresser."

"And you didn't question her about the money?"

"No. I just assumed it was from her job."

"You didn't ask for any?"

"No, I'm fine."

"Fine? What do you do Mr. Park?"

"I'm currently looking for a good position."

Mark David headed for the bedroom. "Mr. Park don't touch anything. Could be evidence. In fact, your entire apartment, with your permission, is sealed off."

"Don't you need a warrant?"

David stopped. "We can get one, if that's what you want. I thought you said you wanted to cooperate?"

"I do. No warrant needed. Go right ahead."

"And we need the keys to your car."

"My car?"

"You okay with that?"

"Yes."

Before anyone had a chance to stop him, Dustin opened the door and walked out onto the balcony. A reflex motion took over Park and he thrust a fist into his mouth to stop a shout. Dustin looked out over Stilton Bay.

"Quite a view you've got here." Dustin could see the Atlantic pushing waves until they became fingers of water and foam bubbles on the sand, reaching up close to a line of sea oats, then absorbed into the billions of beige granules. A light wind bent the tops of a collection of robellini palms, and the air smelled like crushed man-o-wars and near-naked sand-caked bodies from the beach. Dustin kept going until his large frame was up against the railing. All the wind escaped from the lungs of Lucas Park and he couldn't breathe, as he anticipated a city detective falling from the balcony trap he had prepared for his wife.

"Please be careful, I painted some out there." Park warned.

"This view is great." Rather than lean a hand on the rail, Dustin came back inside. "Mr. Park, maybe it would be better if you stayed by the door."

They opened drawers, checked clothing, turned over mattresses, looked into cupboards and went through boxes. And they checked her dresser. No money.

Dustin called for the crime tech team and stepped outside the door where Lucas Park was trying to avoid the eyes of a neighbor.

"We're going to have to be here all day. You have a place to stay?" Dustin was looking toward the street for any sign of the crime techs.

"Not really. I'll probably be at the hospital. Think I'll sleep there."

"Good. If we need you, we'll call you."

Park walked away smiling. He was almost certain they would not look just under the balcony and find the metal box containing the money, strapped to a bolt.

## 22

Mark David led the way into the meeting room. Dustin just behind him. They were not prepared for what they would find. The room was packed. Several lower level staffers were standing along the wall. Every set of eyes bored in on the detectives.

"Come in, gentlemen." Stilton Bay police chief Greg Alter always wore his hat, inside or out. A small patch of gray hair at the temples, Alter wore a uniform a size too small and his stomach was one of the first things you noticed about him. He gestured for the detectives to move to the front. When they maneuvered past the group, Mark David had another surprise. Alter pointed to a man who was standing. "Everyone, Mayor Vernon Thomas."

"Thank you." Thomas wore a suit the color of politician blue. A crisp shirt white against his dark skin. "I'm not going to say much. I'm leaving but I'm leaving everything in the good hands of my executive assistant, Destiny Row. She was tall in her three-inch black heels. She wore a gray plaid suit top, white blouse and matching plaid skirt. The outfit looked warm for Florida, yet inside in the air-conditioning, she would be fine. She pressed a pair of glasses to her face and waited until the mayor left the room before she started talking.

"I've been briefed by the chief," she started. "But the mayor wants to know two things. One, is this contained? And second, is there a suspect?"

The chief turned to the detectives. Mark David spoke. "At this time, we have one victim in the hospital, stable condition suffering from what we believe is poison, after touching a stash of money. We also have a second person who is deceased. The medical examiner confirms she suffered from a touch poison and died within twenty-four hours after, again, touching money."

Row looked over some notes. "Do we think these cases are connected?"

David looked at the chief first, as if looking for permission to respond. "Yes, they could be. We know the deceased was at a location where money was taken from a murder victim. Some of that money was tainted with poison. How that happened, or what type of poison, we just don't know yet. We've ruled out all the major suspects. The M.E. says this is something she's never seen before. The feds are being contacted in terms of what poison it might be."

He waited for a response and saw a room of men and women all taking down notes. The head of his detective unit was there, off in a corner. All members of the unit were present. David looked at Row. He had seen her before on many occasions on television, speaking for the mayor. Her facial expression was all calm, without a hint of what she was thinking. That is, until she spoke. "So, there's two cases, and they still have to be vetted in terms of whether they are connected."

"Yes."

She removed the glasses. "What is your action plan? Aside from finding the killer."

David waited a full ten seconds, waiting for the chief to speak first. When he did not hear anything, he proceeded. "It's the thinking of the M.E. to get the word out. Tell people if they find money or if they picked up any money from that body, they could be putting their lives in danger."

"In danger? Are we sure about that?" The glasses went back on her face.

"This stuff, whatever it is, is a killer. A lot of this cash could have been passed on. Stores, banks, gas stations. Do we want to sit on that?" Mark David waited.

Row folded her hands in front of her. "We don't want to tell you how to do your jobs. That's your department. But if we put this out there, this will be a national story in three seconds. Every news outlet will be here. Our tourism will go south and for what? A single case?"

"Two possible cases. There's a distinct possibility more people will be hurt or killed if we don't put this out to the media." David looked to the chief for support.

She cracked back. "But we don't know that."

David put some oomph into his words. "Someone dies and we don't say anything, it all falls back on the police department."

"You saying the mayor's office is ducking responsibility?"

"I'm just saying if we have a chance to save a life, we should move on that."

She matched the intensity of David's voice. "The mayor doesn't agree. You take your orders from downtown and right now we don't panic anyone!" Her eyes narrowed and a vein in her neck bulged a thick line.

Chief Alter took off his hat. "I think we need to make sure of what we have before we thrust all of this on the public. So, I agree with the mayor's staff. We wait." He turned to David. "Is that clear?"

"Clear, sir."

Destiny Row showed the tiniest bit of a smile and it was gone in less than a second. "Thank you. Let's keep this under wraps for now. I know I'm sounding like some damn fool in a shark movie too scared to make a public statement, but we have to know for sure first before we shake up the city." She headed for the door.

Chief Alter turned to his detectives. "She never got an answer to her second question. Do we have a suspect?"

# 23

"Why didn't you mention Tower?" Sam Dustin tugged on the ragged excuse for a tie and sat on his desk.

"You know there isn't enough to mention him yet." Mark David avoided his stare by going over his list on a pad. "The best thing we can do right now is to keep a watch on him. Tail him if we have to do that, but we can't say he's our number one just yet."

There were four other members of the unit, considered one person too large by the police chief. David argued and fought to keep the staff at the same level. Now he was glad he did and probably needed more help.

Stilton Bay was not large enough for three shifts like other nearby departments. There was just an A and B shift. Alpha-Bravo. The detective unit took on other duties, including robbery, fraud, along with store and home burglaries. Usually, there weren't enough homicides in the city to justify a one-direction unit. This was different. Everything went to the bottom of the stack until the poison death case was solved.

Mark David cleared his throat. "We get any valuable information from the store owners?"

Dustin answered him. "Not much."

"We need to go over things with them again."

"But they don't..."

"Sorry Sam, but we have to pull something out of them. Who were all the people at this thing? How were they contacted? Why didn't anyone call us? Where exactly did the money come from? We have a lot to go through and we're still not certain why this person was shot."

A voice came from the other side of the room. "Could this be a professional hit? They picked up their own casings."

Mark David put his pad down. "Think about it. A pro wouldn't leave money behind. They would never go through all this trouble of staging the body and calling people to the park. It just doesn't fit. And in our experience, how many hitters move the body once the hit has been done?"

Silence.

He started in again with more questions. "When we were out there, anyone see any drag marks? I mean, how did the body get there?"

"The problem is," Dustin started, "the beach. Someone could walk along the beach line and never leave any footprints. There are no cameras in that section and again, the one camera we have there, doesn't work. My bet is they used the beachfront."

Mark David wrote down some notes. "And the missing bullets from the body. Even without them, maybe the examiner can find traces of the bullet and give us some direction. And the size of the entry wound could tell us something." He pointed to a member of his team. "You want to check on that? Correct that. I'll do it myself."

Dustin wiped his brow. "Without those bullets, we can't do a gun match. Pretty gory stuff for a killer to dig them out."

"Generally, hitmen don't do that. Why take the time?" Mark David reasoned.

Throughout his time on the force, David always thought the police building itself was out of place. Built in the wrong location. Police HQ was far north of the downtown pavilion where the body was discovered. More than once, merchants asked, then demanded the town put in a sub-station closer to the business community. The requests and demands were always turned down. Now Mark David was again considering if things would be much different if they were located closer to the beach area.

He doled out other assignments. The IT department was given the task of looking for other homicide cases across the state and country dealing with a killer who removed bullet fragments from the body. Another detective was directed to look at recent visitors to the area, hotels and boat marinas. Mark David wrote – MOTIVE – at the top of his pad and circled the word three times. With motive, he told the group, a killer would emerge.

He tried to shrug off what he sometimes called The Big R. In David's world, the big R stood for responsibility. People were dying on his watch. Shot and poisoned. And he had reason to believe others could be harmed. The city, the mayor, the police chief were all counting on his people to find the killer or killers. Yet throughout it all, he had just one real concern. From what all the facts were telling them, there would, in time, be another victim.

## 24

---

Lucas Park tried to pinpoint the exact time when he decided to kill his wife. He sat by her hospital bed, watching Joni connected to a ventilator. Maybe, he thought, she could just pass in the night. Quiet, and out of his life forever. She was sleeping. Monitors were in the room, checking her blood pressure and heart. Doctors had taken her blood on three separate occasions, looking for any change in her health. Tests were being made to check the type of poison.

Still, all Park wanted to do was disconnect all of the machinery. Too many witnesses, he concluded. The question remained fixed on his current thoughts. Killing his wife. His hands gripped the arms of the chair. Thoughts moved through him, thinking about the incident four years earlier when she publicly chastised him in front of friends. She called him lazy and not man enough to get a good job. Joni later said the four glasses of wine made her say things she regretted. Yet, that wasn't the turning-point moment. What about the time she called the cable company to end their service, just as he was about to see the final installment of a critically acclaimed TV series. She yelled at him that she wanted to reduce costs and he wasn't contributing to the bills. Five different times, she hid the TV remote saying he needed to spend time looking for work, rather than wasting time in front of the television.

He knew the moment.

On the one rare vacation, just one in the past eight years, while visiting the Bahamas, she left without him. Joni paid the hotel bill, got on a plane and left him without saying a word. He had to call his brother, get money wired to him so he could buy the short trip flight to Fort Lauderdale and the quick ride to Stilton Bay. When he finally walked in the door, she screamed at him for stealing money from her purse and losing the entire lot in the casino. He tried to deny it all, but the humiliation of calling his brother stuck with him like a bad dream. To this day, he still owed his sibling the money. His shock came when the hotel informed him he no longer had a room. Lucas just stood there and lied, saying he was the victim of a robbery. When police confronted him with hours of video showing he was on a loser's streak at the casino, he yielded and asked for public assistance to get home. He was given a free phone call to reach anyone he wanted in the world. In short, they treated him with excellent service, showing him all the courtesy they could to a man without a single dollar to his name.

From the horrendous moments in the hotel, the showdown with police, calling his brother, waiting at the airport and the flight home, all Lucas Park thought about was how to end her life.

Now, he had his wish gift-wrapped. The doctors told him about the possible poison connection and that in most cases, there was almost no hope. By morning, Joni Park would die. The corners of his mouth bent upwards in the wicked smile he usually kept to himself, alone with his thoughts on how to dispatch her. Everything was perfect. The insurance money would be his and when the killer was finally caught, maybe even a wrongful death lawsuit.

The smile evaporated when two rather large Stilton Bay police officers took up a position just outside Joni's door.

He leaned over her. "You're just where you need to be. Close to death. And away from me. You were a pain in the ass and all I do is think of how to murder you."

His words were interrupted by the arrival of a doctor. She made a direct path to Park after a quick glance at Joni. "Mr. Park?"

"Yes."

"You okay? You shouldn't worry, she's in good hands."

"No, I'm fine. I just want her to pull through. I miss her." He turned to the door.

She followed his gaze to the police officers. "They were ordered to be here." The doctor looked down at the floor, then back up to Park. "We still don't know what caused this. We are in the midst of a search for the exact poison that put her in the hospital." The doctor studied Joni, then looked back at Park.

"I'm prepared for her death," he told her. "I know how these things go and I am ready to let her go. She can move on to the next world in dignity. Her autopsy might even help with the investigation."

The doctor put a hand on his shoulder. "I'm glad you are prepared. However, I am pleased to tell you the words I know you want to hear. From what we can tell, we got to her in time and we think she's going to recover from this and be just fine."

"What?"

# 25

---

"What's new?" Mark David's movements were in quick motion, signs of a person who didn't have much time. He called using live video so they could see each other.

"And hello to you." Elly Kent's words were smothered in sarcasm.

"Sorry, I'm doing a hundred things."

"I wouldn't bother you unless it was important."

"Okay."

She adjusted her body and took in a deep breath as if ready to make a speech. "There's a lot. First, a team from the C.D.C. might be coming in the next few days. Second, this thing doesn't act like ricin. With ricin, it has to be inhaled or ingested. The delivery agent is touch, I'm sure of it."

"In itself, that's scary."

"From what I could see, Pam Oakman didn't have any cuts on her. Normally, ricin could enter the body through a cut. But the paramedics told me later, that they found money in her bra."

"That's not in my notes." Mark David sounded concerned.

"That's why I called you. You should know all this right away." She started to whisper. "Someone has found a way to deliver this poison a different way, by simple touch. I think a person has to really rub it on their body, otherwise simply handling it might not be fatal."

"Our second victim, Joni Park is going to make it. At least that's what the doctors think. I'm hoping to talk to her as soon as she wakes up. I've got officers at her hospital room."

She sounded like she was pleading. "Good. What about warning the public?"

Detective Mark David went silent. He turned away from the phone, thinking about downtown, where the body was found. He didn't have an answer for her. On the other line, Kent balled up her fist. "You mean those sorry-asses are sitting and doing nothing while people could be the next to die?"

"I tried..."

"Tried? You don't know where that money is right now. A child could be playing with that money as we speak. Banks could be handing out that money."

David gripped the writing pad until the thing almost bent. "I plan to call the chief again. Make another plea. You're right. This has to get out to the public."

"I could do it." Her voice was firm.

"Don't. You got passed over for head of your unit the last time you spoke out."

"I don't care. You've got twenty-four hours. If your office doesn't let the public know about this, I will." She started to hang up, stopped and thought about her next move. "I'm worried about you Mark. If we weren't so busy, I'd ask you to dinner."

"You sure we could make it work this time?"

She stayed silent.

He noticed a bag in the corner of the room. "Got a body in there?"

She laughed. "Naw, just some camping and climbing gear. I've been promising myself to get out of the state. I was just about to do that when all this happened."

"You didn't answer my question. About us doing something together again."

She stared at him the way two lovers do when they want to communicate without talking. "Maybe we could try. If you were here, I'd kiss you."

"Why?"

"Just about every available guy in this town runs from me when they find out what I do for a living. Everyone, except you." A few seconds passed with Elly staring at him. "You weren't afraid of me. Even the guys in college ran like ants on fire. Take care, Mark David."

"I will."

# 26

With two lights burned out, the front of the building was encased in shadow. Frank Tower hesitated at first, deciding whether to go inside or drive off. He got out of the car and stood, taking in the ambiance of the parking lot. One window in the long structure was lit. There was no one in the lobby or at the front desk. Tower saw just enough light to make out the sign mounted on the top of the place: NEVER TOO LATE.

He watched a single figure walking to the front door. When she emerged he felt no emotion, other than a lack of comfort, almost to the level of disdain for the woman who was now just a few feet from him.

"No hello for your mother?"

"Evening Jackie."

A weak smile line stretched across the dry lips. "My Frankie!" She ventured to get closer, not sure of the reaction. "Can I hug you?"

"Let's just skip the hugs, okay?"

The smile evaporated. "I understand."

Jackie waited, as if not sure what to do next.

Tower almost turned to leave. This was the woman who left him alone for hours when he was a mere three years old to score crack cocaine. The same woman who saved for months to buy him a birthday present, only to take the money instead to binge on drugs. She was the person who made a decision years ago that drugs would rule her life, breaking into homes was the priority to buy more mind-soaking crack, rather than raise a tyke named Frank Boyd Tower. And yes, this was the very one who now asked permission for a hug.

Tower leaned against his car. "You've got some lights out."

"I know. Been meaning to fix up the place. Needs paint'n too. I've got seventeen clients in there, all drug-free, just like me. They need the help I'm giving them. The best drug rehab center in Stilton Bay. I'm proud of my place."

Tower thought she held up remarkably well, considering she had spent a large part of her life putting crap into her body. There were just a few face wrinkles and a hint of sparkle still left in the brown eyes. The damage was in the hair. She kept everything pulled back, her once glossy black strands now mixed with a lot of white, like streaks of lightning on a dark sky.

Tower asked, "You still got the separate living quarters in the back?"

"Yeah, it's there. You need it?"

Over the years, after her addiction was under control and she cleaned up, Tower tried to find the way to resolve his low-burn anger over the way he was treated as a child. Fighting an empty stomach, he once ate wood chips for food, with the stench of soiled trainer pants, crying for hours until the tears went dry, banging on the door for a neighbor's help that didn't come. He had never called her mother, resorting instead to just address her by the one name. Jackie.

"Okay Jackie if I use it for a few days?"

"Sure Frankie. Anything you want." She reached into a back pocket and threw him the keys. "You got a home and a wife. You have a falling out with Shannon?"

"We're fine. I just need a place to lay low for a few days, that's all."

"The only thing I ask is, in the morning, be careful around my clients. One look at you and they'll think they're going to jail. You still look like a cop."

"I'll be out and about during the day. I promise."

"I love you, Frankie."

"Bye Jackie."

Her head shook with the thoughts running through her so hard, her left eye twitched. "Frankie, I'm still trying to find ways to say I'm sorry."

"Bye Jackie," he said a bit louder.

"Please, Frankie." She waved her arm at the Never Too Late. "All this is a way to show you I've changed."

Tower kept moving on.

"Frankie!"

Tower didn't so much as watch her go back inside. He got back into his car and drove around to the back of the Never Too Late. The facility was the end result of three years, convincing the city, drug users, and herself to open the place. She was the owner and still owed sixteen years on the mortgage.

When Tower drove around, there was even less light in the back parking lot. Off, in a wooded section, was a three-bedroom house. When her place filled up, Jackie wanted a hide-away, a place to stay. For now, this would be home for Frank Tower.

He turned on the lights. The house was small but clean. The Never Too Late was just east of I-95, the state road running north and south through Florida, down into Fort Lauderdale and on to Miami. Stilton Bay was just south of Deerfield Beach. The rehab center was secluded next to the Interstate and Tower could see the lights from the cars thirty feet up and hear the noise from thousands driving back and forth.

The place was in the heart of the T-Town section of the city, where pimps found a landing place and women sold themselves on the street. T-Town got its name because all the streets started with the letter T. Drugs were an easy get. Tower settled in for the night, taking up a room with a view of the back walkway. He wanted peace and away from the spotlight of a murder investigation.

# 27

Harsh yellow and crimson flared between the blades of the window blinds. Cason Willow always kept the blinds closed otherwise the morning sunlight caused one to raise a hand to the face to ward off the rays. His clock showed 8:38 A.M. Willow was just ready to enter the shower when the text message lit up his phone.

CLUSTER BASH.

For Willow, the two words meant another secret text from the same person or persons who sent him on the trek where he found a body. Under cluster bash, he found the following:

DON'T HESITATE. MORE MONEY. BE THERE OR BE PREPARED TO MISS OUT. DETAILS ON THE LOCATION IN THIRTY MINUTES.

He hid the message from Sonia. She was already up and cooking breakfast. Forty questions lit up his thoughts. Should he finally call the police? Tell Sonia? Should he go? Maybe this time, it will be just money, he thought. No body.

The depths of one's guilt might be confined to a person's capacity to do what is right. Willow considered what guilt he shared in the finding of a body and the money. He just thought his guilt was very limited since he did not kill anyone and he took only a small amount of cash. The weight on him was always the fact he did not contact the police. Even now, he figured many others received the same phone message. Why can't they contact the authorities? For days he scoured the newspapers online and found almost no mention of the body, other than the first couple of days. Money found on the street, was money found. Why not go for it again? The side of him to take the money again was winning.

The sounds and smells of fine chopped onions with potatoes and eggs carried to the bedroom where Willow agonized on what do. He showered, dressed and sat down at the table.

"Anything I should know?" Sonia Mason stared at him while placing a glass of orange juice next to the plate.

"Know? I'm fine."

"I know you too well, Cason Willow. There's something bothering you." She put together her own plate, never letting her eyes stray away from Willow.

"Just something I'm thinking about."

Like a twelve-year-old with a penchant for saving things, Willow kept the money from the dead man stashed in a metal box tucked under his bed. He wanted the money separate from his life, with some distance and not part of the regular world. He kept waiting for the police to smash down the door and throw him in cuffs. Nothing happened, leaving Willow to think the money was finders-keepers. His eyes remained transfixed on his phone. Wherever the next message sent him, he had to be ready.

"I scored an A on the last test," he said, changing the subject.

"Great. A means you don't have to drop the class."

"No, I think I'll be okay." He was now ready for the lie.

In the two years together, Willow had fibbed just twice. He forgot the anniversary of their first date and told her a gift was coming. A lie. A friend gave him a present to give her and Willow had no idea what was inside the box. The six scarves were a surprise to both Willow and Sonia. The second was a traffic citation for speeding. He had to attend four classes, and he explained they were business meetings. This would be the third.

"I have to study late tonight." He waited for her response.

"No problem. Gives me a chance to catch up on a few things and not worry about dinner. Don't wake me up when you get in."

Willow smiled the smile of a liar. A few seconds later, guilt washed over him like a hurricane storm surge.


Lucas Park sat in the lobby of the hospital, in deep thought. If Joni woke up and told police her version of what happened, the story would not match his own. Detectives would know immediately he was not telling the truth and he would be a suspect.

Two Stilton Bay officers remained at her door. The urge to do something was imperative. Somehow, he reasoned, she would have to die. Now. He went over the latest details from the doctor. The poison destroyed one kidney, but she could live with the other. There was also liver damage, but she could survive that as well. The fluid in her lungs was under control, although she would need help breathing for the next several weeks. The ordeal would take time, but she would one day leave the hospital and lead a near normal life.

"Shit," Park whispered to himself. How could he change all that? He was so involved in what to do, several minutes passed before he finally noticed he had a phone message. A text. He couldn't contain the smile. Another money drop. Still, the message did not say where or when, just to keep looking for another message. Park left the hospital. He was forming a new plan. One without Joni. If he could secure enough money, he would just leave. No matter what amount he got, Park was prepared to get out of Stilton Bay.

For one, he would arrive early. Maybe he could get to the exact spot before anyone else. Second, he would get gloves and an inner liner inside his clothing. He thought about the risk of reaching for money that might be soaked in poison.

Lucas Park didn't care.

He got into his car and continued to concentrate on everything he needed before the next message arrived.

# 28

Frank Tower moved about his office like a caged tiger. He had a list of things he could do to investigate the claims against him. There were people he would interview, locations to photograph. Yet, he stayed in his office, writing out his own investigative notes and for the second time in his life, he was forced to clear himself. The first was the incident of the stolen money somewhere between a crime scene and the evidence room. He went out of his way to make sure everyone saw him. Before he left the Never Too Late, he dropped in at the front desk and spoke with the receptionist. On the way to the office, he stopped for gas, speaking with the attendant and looking directly into the camera in the corner. When he got to his office, Tower made sure his neighbors all saw him and made a long conversation talking about football. Throughout the morning, Tower left little footprints of an alibi all over Stilton Bay just in case he needed to provide authorities information on his journey.

While in the office, he left a message for Shannon. He still did not want to inform her of the death. She was busy at the conference and he promised he would not husband-stalk her while she was away.

Finally, he left a message for Mark David. He just wanted his former partner to know he was in the office if he was needed. Tower felt like a man on parole. A man who had to check in every now and then. Outside, cars passed, an easy breeze tilted the tops of the magnolia trees on the swale.

He felt trapped.

He went over the evidence against him. He could try to explain how his fingerprints ended up on a dead man. The transfer of a fingerprint has been known for many years. What he couldn't figure out is why Kulis Barney? What was his connection to the killer? And more so, why was Tower a target?

One clear thing working in his favor is lack of motive. With all the evidence pointing to himself, there was no clear path to connect all the dots leading to why Tower would kill anyone. He was hoping the homicide unit would see things the same way. For now, he would let the homicide boys run the show.

Tower never got a warning from police to stay around, yet he stayed in the city. He had six hours or so to go and he would stop for a sandwich and head to the small house behind the rehabilitation center. Just one more night, he reasoned. One night of acting like a criminal on the run and then he was going to go full-throttle Tower. One night to give the police a chance to strike his name from the suspect list or he would do it himself, his way. The Tower way.

# 29

Vera Rossin ran the hallway ignoring the flapping sides of her white lab coat. She was a rambling collection of loose parts of bouncing hair, shoes almost coming off, bracelet sliding up and down her arm and two pens falling out of her pocket. Rossin was in full gallop down the pristine white floors of the Stilton Bay medical examiner's office. When she reached the office of Elly Kent, Rossin was out of breath. She flung the door open, catching Kelly on the phone. She stopped talking.

"What is it?" Kelly's eyes widened as she took in the disheveled Rossin.

"I just heard..." Rossin couldn't finish the sentence. She bent over and sucked in air.

"I just heard on the street..."

"Heard what!" Kelly got up from her desk and got in Rossin's face. "What happened?"

Rossin stood up. "They were talking about it. A text message about a lot of money."

"Who was saying this?"

"I didn't see their faces; I was rounding the corner and I just heard a male and female voice talking about it."

"They say where?" Kelly was picking up the phone while taking in everything Rossin was saying.

"No, just that they were waiting for more information."

"Thanks Vera." Kelly had the phone pressed to her ear. "Mark David please. Yes, I'll hold."

In less than fifteen minutes, Mark David was at the ME office, interviewed Rossin and was making phone calls for any surveillance video in the area. "You remember anything else? Like where they were headed?"

Rossin rubbed her forehead. "No. I just got the feeling they didn't know where to go just yet. But they were excited." She looked around the room, then back to David. "I'm sorry I can't give you anything more. As she moved her arms, the bracelet made a soft hollow rattle sound.

"That's okay. This helps us tremendously. Thanks for your help."

Rossin stepped back and left the office. Mark David pulled out his cell phone. "I'm coming back to the office. We have to get some things set up. And right now."

Mark David stepped into a room with a noise level far above the norm. Three people who normally would be off, were called back to duty. Two desks were formed into a make-shift war room with chairs arranged around them. The white board was filled with pictures of the dead victim, the one in the hospital and photographs of the crime scene where the money was found. Dustin waved in his direction. When he got to the huddle, he stood next to Randell Stemple, the I.T. director. They were looking at a large computer monitor.

"What have we got?" Mark David reached for his notepad.

Stemple pointed to the screen. "We're all over the place. After your phone call, we reached out to as many people as we could to just tell us if they received any text message with information about a money pick up."

"Couldn't we just monitor cell phones?" Dustin asked.

Stemple was in heavy thought. "We could, but we need a court order. And what number? We don't have a target yet."

Mark David stopped writing down info. "What about buying some phones? We don't know how these people were picked out to get the messages in the first place."

"I'll call. Get a requisition for burner phones."

"If I can interject." Stemple rested his hands on the keyboard. "From what we know, we should be going back to all those we discovered were at the first scene. See if they are getting new hits on their phone to come to another location."

"I'm on it." Mark David moved to his desk, looking through the folder for phone numbers. In the past day, they were able to contact four other people who came forward with money. So far, none of them showed any signs of being poisoned. "What about the news media?" David shouted. "I think the public needs to know that if they see money out there, it could kill them."

"Stand down from that idea." Destiny Row was wearing a khaki skirt and white blouse. Her glasses were mounted on top of her head, like a crown. "We work silently, but without alarming the public. This comes from your chief and the mayor." Following her into the room was Chief Alter, looking downward like a man without any support.

The noise in the room abated. Mark David turned to her. "Is it the mayor's position to stand by and say nothing while a public threat could kill people?"

"We don't know that yet." Row stopped and stood just behind Stemple. She looked over his shoulder at the monitor. "No court orders, no public statements. Nothing. We do this in silent mode, is that clear? Nothing public."

Dustin spoke up. "And chief, you signed off on this?"

Chief Alter could barely be heard. "I think it's in the best interest to follow this course."

Row snapped at Dustin. "You questioning me, Mr. Dustin? You with the less than stellar career sheet. Yes, I read yours. And I read the history of everyone in this room. No one. Not you Mr. Dustin, not anyone moves to the public with this unless I say so."

The group saw her back as she left the room with the chief following like a duckling behind its mother.

David refused to be defeated. "Well, that's it. No court order. However, start making phone calls."

# 30

Lucas Park saw the incoming caller ID message as coming from the police department and ignored the ring. He had a more important task at hand. The trunk door of his car was in the raised position. Park studied his work. Two empty backpacks were tucked to the side. He devised a plan to stuff both packs with money, making it easier to carry than just using his hands. There was also a miner's flashlight on a strap he would attach to his forehead, a folded knife, three pairs of plastic gloves and two anti-fume masks to cover his nose and mouth. Park smiled. He was ready.

He glanced around every few minutes to see if anyone was monitoring him. While he moved about the car, Park never took his eyes off the phone, always looking for a message.

The message.

He took out a bag and pressed his fingers into the clear packaging. Inside, were three new burner phones, all purchased from different locations, with Park turning his head away from the store surveillance cameras as much as possible. If he was able to snare a great deal of money, he intended to smash his phone and rely only on the burners. He wanted to get rid of his driver's license and credit cards to help start his new life. A life without his wife. Dead or alive.

No matter what happened in the next twenty-four hours, Lucas Park was committed to leaving Stilton Bay. He wasn't facing a crime. This was still America and he could go where he wanted, do anything and yes, abandon Joni. If that was his wish, well, so be it. And Park was sure of another thing if he left. Starting a new life would mean working, perhaps for the first real time. Again, so be it. He glanced at his watch. 10:56 P.M. He sat in his car, behind the wheel, all gassed up and ready to go in any direction. He just needed to know where.

He was near the site where the body was found. There was a boost in the pungent odor of brine-scented sea air. The wind had kicked up and a row of canopy tops began to sway and lift. He could hear the breeze rattling layers of palm fronds, kicking them together until they were making their own song. Park feared next would come rain. He did not need all the wetness for what he was about to do. A spread of red-seared clouds pressed against the dark sky like they were hot coals. Then, as if Park had ordered it himself, the winds calmed and the sense of impending rain went away. He sat up in the seat.

The message on his phone was short.

WELCOME TO NIGHT MONEY

GO TO CLAXTON AND 5$^{TH}$. THE MONEY IS NOT THERE. BUT DETAILS

TO COME.

Park started the engine. Time to move. Purpose was in front of him. He glided out of the parking spot quiet like a knife being pulled from a sheath. Quiet and easy, as if he wanted no one to know he was leaving.

# 31

Cason Willow was running to his car. He had no idea how many people got the same information. He brought a duffle bag with him. There was a moment when he thought about calling Sonia, spill everything, and let her know he was about to do something stupid. Again. He decided against calling her and drove off in the direction of Claxton and 5$^{th}$. He was just hoping he would not be the last one there.

There was a different pulse moving through Willow. A new tone of attitude and vision, one with a purpose without guilt. He was driving faster than his usual speed, caring less about others. He had lied to Sonia without any remorse. He promised himself he would call police about the money and never did. This was a turning point in his life. The possibility of grabbing a lot of free money was taking him down a new path and Willow didn't fight it, letting the pulse take over his body.

Willow hesitated for the last time. This trip would not be a repeat. He promised himself to be aggressive, push past others, take the lead, and shut down anyone in his way.

He zoomed past buildings in downtown Stilton Bay, past the college where he studied, past the old Franklin's store that was now an Internet café, past the collection of tourist shops and restaurants, all now closed.

Two red lights did not slow him down. Willow drove through the intersections with no intention of slowing down or letting a mere red light stand in the way of getting to the location. In fifteen minutes, Willow slowed down as he approached Claxton. There was an empty building where a store outlet that went bankrupt, had a large parking lot. Willow pulled in. He parked near another car. The driver of the car appeared to view him nervously. The man was wearing gloves.

Each time the driver of the other car turned to look in his direction, Willow turned away or ducked down.


Lucas Park was suspicious of the car and the driver who kept ducking down toward the wheel. For Park, the figure did not look like a police officer. He had a few options. Park could ignore the other driver, leave and come back in a few minutes or confront the man. Park was feeling exceptionally powerful. He opened the door, stepped out and leaned against the car, staring in the direction of the other driver.


Willow recognized the man getting out of the car. This was the same man who pushed past him for the money. Willow got out of the car and stood, staring at the man, who was reorganizing things in the front seat. For no reason he could figure, Willow started walking toward him.


Park wasn't quite sure what to do. He started to look for a weapon as the man approached him. He changed his mind and stood to face him.

"You were there the last time." Willow said.

Park hesitated at first. "Yeah, I was there."

Willow checked the front seat of the car. "That's a lot of stuff."

"Got more in the trunk." Park looked at the entrance to the parking lot. "So, you didn't call police?"

"No. Did you?"

Park smiled, revealing the partial green molar in the back of his mouth. "You got the same message I did."

Willow nodded. "No reason to work against each other. Hopefully, there's plenty more money." As he talked, Willow watched Park open the trunk of the car. His jaw dropped open just a bit, as he examined the contents of medical masks and backpacks.

There was a certain glow of pride on Park's face. "I came prepared."

Willow picked up the mask. "What's this for?"

Park took the mask from Willow. "You mean you didn't hear about the poison?"

"Did you say, poison?"

# 32

Mark David stood in the middle of a torrent of motion. Detectives were moving past him in tiny missed collisions as the room was very active. "I want the helicopter on stand-by," David shouted. "If we get word of a lot of people on the roads, going in a certain direction, I want them followed from the air." As he spoke, people were taking down notes. "Patrol got the word at shift change. Yes, we don't quite know what we're looking for, but everyone is on alert."

He looked at a map of the city. "What about the unit watching Frank Tower?" Dustin turned from his computer. "They say he hasn't moved. Staying at the rehab center."

"Okay," David shouted. "Stay with him." He went down a list on a pad. "What about Lucas Park? We heard from him?"

Again, Dustin answered. "Nothing. We went by his place and his car is gone."

"I want him found."

I.T. expert Randell Stemple approached David. "We are hearing rumors of a text message but we don't have anything official."

"Same area as the tip from Rossin?"

"Yeah, I think so. We got patrols all over that section of the city."

"Good." Mark David rubbed his chin as if there was something he was missing, some point of Stilton Bay that needed his attention. He looked at the list in front of him. Traffic was able to determine the license plates of seven cars where the body was found. All seven owners were contacted and claimed they did not have any money. None of them turned up in the hospital. David did not have enough units to sit on their homes at the moment. He was tempted to just pick up the phone and call a reporter. There was a growing sense the public needed to be told what they could face.

"I could use Tower." Mark David's comment wasn't heard by the group. In his heart, he knew Tower wasn't a viable threat to anyone. More than anything, a Frank Tower on the force, coupled with David's own talents and anything could be accomplished. Their short career together weighed on him and he wanted the chance again to go over case notes with him. Just not yet.

Stemple shouted out to the room. "I'll check our street cameras. See what I can find."

"Great, thanks." David turned to his partner. "Do you actually think that if people knew this money could kill them, that they would still snatch it up?"

"In a word, for some, yes. If there was any chance they would get away with it, then yeah, I think people would reach over a dead body for poison-tainted money."

David shrugged. "I think you're right."

## 33

Several cars showed up at the parking lot. Willow recognized them as being at the sight of the body. Now, more cars were arriving. He looked at Park. "You're saying some of that money was poisoned?"

"My wife is in the hospital right now. Police say the money almost killed her. Did you hear about a woman named Pam Oakman? She died in her shop, not far from here."

"You mean her too?"

"Dead. You won't hear about it on the news, but she was a victim." Park studied Willow. "So, are you so anxious to get at that money now?"

"How does...I mean, how could anyone get poison on the money? You sure it's from the money?"

"I'm positive. Not sure on the how part."

Willow stared off toward the red clouded sky. "I touched that money. Handled it. My girlfriend touched it. Nothing happened to us."

"From what I understand, not all the money is bad. Just some of it." Park watched more cars arrive. "And these fools don't even know. Cops are keeping it secret."

Willow looked at his hands. "That's why you have gloves in the car. And the mask."

"I'm still going after the money, but I'm taking precautions."

"That makes us sound desperate."

There was an edge in Park's voice. "So, when we get this next text, you're just going to sit there and let everyone else race to the money."

Willow grimaced. "We took that money off a dead man."

Park was not good at waiting. He had to work at it like a job, taking moments of freaking out and letting things smooth out. He got out of his car and walked a short distance, then back to the car. He had to remain as focused as planning the death of his wife. When he was focused, time went by quickly. Every few steps of his walk, Park stared at his cell phone. On his third trip in a small area, he ended up in front of Cason. He pointed a finger at him.

"That money was left there for us to find. Period."

Four cars drove away, tires peeling, spitting rocks. Park looked at his phone. "Dammit." He moved behind the wheel.

Willow checked his phone. There was a new message.

THE MONEY IS YOURS. ALL OF IT.

T-TOWN. TREMMEL AVENUE AND THOMAS STREET.

Willow slid behind the wheel and followed Park and the other cars. A caravan of automobiles all headed for the bad side of the tracks in Stilton Bay.

## 34

Jackie couldn't sleep. The demons of her drug past sometimes haunted her in the evening hours, when her urges once made her disavow everything in her life except crack. She rolled over in bed a few times, throwing the covers to the floor trying to keep her eyes closed. During these times, her dreams were chopped up episodes of scoring drugs and thinking she would return to her run-down apartment to find the body of young Frankie, alone and abandoned. In one nightmare, the crack was always just beyond her outstretched hands; always running for something she couldn't grasp. They would always be with her, the feeling of taking in the crack, an accomplishment of self-destruction, giving over her mind to a chemical, erasing good memories and replacing them with only the momentary exhilaration the drug could bring.

She sat up in bed, covered in a sweat. Jackie wiped down her face, turned the pillow to the cool side and lowered her head to the fold. The wall lit up with headlights. First, one set, then another. When she opened her eyes, the entire wall was aglow with moving balls of light. She heard cars pulling into the driveway with people getting out, slamming doors and walking around with flashlights.

As she did every time she woke, Jackie said a soft thank-you to herself, counting the days of being clean. No more drugs, no abandoning anyone.

The road to drug-free-day took many turns with three attempts at withdrawal. There were many more times when the taste of the drug was on her tongue and all she had to do was pick up the phone and in minutes, she could get a hookup. Just call. All of it ended. The only exhilaration now, came from seeing others pull themselves from the shit-pit of a drug habit.

Jackie pulled on jeans and a top, then ran to the front door. She counted perhaps fifteen automobiles in the lot. There was a stirring within the bowels of The Never Too Late. Clients were heard moving about in their rooms. Lights came on. A few doors popped open, with worried faces staring into the hallway.

Jackie tried to sound soothing. "Don't worry, I'll check it out. It's not a raid. Go back to bed." Doors closed. Jackie was now in full fast-walk to the front door. She unlocked the tall glass doors and walked out into the parking lot. No one was approaching her center. Instead, people were walking in and around the lot, looking down, searching for something. When she approached, they moved away from her.

"What are you looking for?" She shouted. "This is my place. What do you want?"

No one answered.

Lucas Park stood just a few feet from Willow. Instead of rushing around like the others, Park waited. "Something is wrong."

Willow was impatient. "What if they get to it first. We could lose out."

"I'm telling ya, something is wrong. Once we got to T-Town, we got a message to come here. And there's nothing." Park looked right to left, sizing up the crowd of money hunters.

Jackie moved directly into the path of several beams coming from flashlights and demanded. "What are ya'll looking for? Why are you here?"

Willow walked up to her. "Sorry to bother you but we were told..." he hesitated. "Can we look around?"

"No!" Jackie started walking until she blocked the way of two men and a woman headed for the back of the place. "You are all trespassing and unless you leave in the next thirty seconds, I'm calling the police."

From his unmarked car, detective Grayson Olson watched the horde of cars and people filling up the parking lot of the Never Too Late. People were all around him, bouncing out of cars and looking puzzled. He almost got out himself until there was a knock on his driver's side window. Olson stared into the face of Frank Tower.

"Olson, right?" Tower watched the window roll down. "Been with homicide long?"

"I'm not supposed to talk to you." Olson fidgeted in the seat.

"Yeah, I know. You're supposed to be doing surveillance on me. I know the drill." Tower pointed to the mass confusion in front of the Never Too Late. "You better tell your boss to get down here."

# 35

Detective Mark David's car rolled to a stop next to Olson. He got out of the car waving his hands. "So, where is everybody?" David checked his watch. 11:37 P.M.

"They're gone." Olson looked like the shepherd who was missing his flock. "When someone mentioned Tower, they bolted."

David looked around the place. Tower stepped forward. "In case you're wondering, there are no cameras here. Jackie won't have it. Says it works against the whole vibe of the place."

Again, David turned his attention to Olson. "You get any plates?"

"They moved too fast."

Tower bored a stare into Mark David. "They were all here looking for something. Just like the night they found the body. Same circumstances."

Mark David walked the perimeter twice, looking through the bushes, aiming his flashlight up and down the swale. Nothing. He had one more question for Olson. "Tower been here all night?"

"Far as I know, yeah."

"Go home."

Olson fired up the engine and drove off. Mark David looked squarely into the stare of his former partner. "You know this is routine. That I have to find a way to move you off suspicion. And the best way to do that is follow your ass."

Tower said, "We both know it's B.S. but I'm trying to be out in the open. I have nothing to hide. With Shannon out of town, I wanted some witnesses around me. So, I'm here."

"You talk to any of them?"

"The people tonight? No. But they were clearly looking for something."

Mark David walked back to his car and checked in with his office before leaving.

Willow found a corner of a gas station parking lot and waited. He sat in his car for twenty minutes deciding what to do next. He was confused. Why would anyone send them to a location where nothing was happening? Right now, the only solution was to wait for another text message. A message that did not come. He went over all the steps again, thinking maybe he got the information wrong. If that was the case, everyone got it wrong. They were sent to the wrong place on purpose. He drove toward his apartment. Three turns later, he did not notice the car following him. Willow did not want to return empty-handed. He had no other choice. Once parked, he checked the phone one last time. Nothing new. He went upstairs into the apartment.

Lucas Park stayed back a fair distance to keep himself hidden from Willow, yet he could see all movements. He pulled out a pair of binoculars and watched Willow go into the apartment building. There was no lock on the door. When Willow checked his mailbox, Park took notice of the number. The binoculars let him see that close. Willow disappeared into the elevator. Park remembered the information.

"If I need to find you, I know where you live," he whispered to himself.

# 36

All the windows were open in the third-floor apartment of Sola Johnson. She liked it that way. Her two-bedroom apartment faced the beaches of Stilton Bay, one of the most coveted places to live in town. The ocean breezes made her smile and so the windows stayed open.

2:45 A.M. Johnson thought she heard noises coming from the beach. She got up. "There can't be anybody out there," she whispered to her cat, Hercules. The cat propped himself on the ledge, probably not wanting to use up those cat lives if he got any closer to the long drop below. She looked out the window. There were several voices coming from below, across the street, on the sand. She focused her attention until she spotted more than a dozen people fighting over something. There were arms flailing in the air, shouts of unrest and people knocking others to the ground. One man swearing so loud, she could make out the words. Clearly, she could see at least three separate fights, with people trying to get a firm stance in the shifting sands in order to land a punch. She could just make out a form on the sand, not moving. And they were pulling what looked like stacks of paper from the clothing of the figure. It was clearer now. Her jaw dropped like a puppet's mouth with the strings cut.

They were fighting over money.

One person kicked another down. Two more were stuffing bills in their shirts, while a third was jamming wads of cash into a purse. Johnson reached for the phone, dropping the thing twice before dialing 9-1-1.

"911, is this an emergency?"

"Yes," Johnson stammered. "The scarecrow is dead."

"What? Scarecrow? Is everything okay there? Are you hurt?"

Johnson tried to give a description. "They're attacking him. He looks like a scarecrow with all the stuffing. The stuffing is money and they are fighting and taking it. But the scarecrow is dead!"

"Where is this happening?"

"Down on the beach. I'm on the third floor. Someone killed the scarecrow."

"I have your address in the system. So, you are safe?"

"Yes, I'm fine. I don't think they see me but you better get some help."

"How many people are there?"

"I'm guessing a dozen." Johnson paused. The smattering of people started to scatter like roaches. "They're all leaving. Hurry if you want to catch anyone." One person was still picking at the bills, plucking them from around the man's neck. The others were gone, running toward A1A, the street that lines the beach. Johnson could not find any cars, just the sounds of people running.

"Git here quick. There's just one person left," Johnson said. "And the scarecrow."

# 37

---

Mark David looked at the pattern of footsteps in the sand and shook his head. "This isn't going to be easy." A long line of police crime tape and four uniforms kept the public off the beach. Sam Dustin wiped down his face for the third time. "I didn't get much sleep," he said. He checked his phone. 4:20 A.M.

The body was face up, eyes open, with a ripped shirt, open pants and one missing shoe. "They really got into him," Dustin moved out of the way to make room for two more crime techs.

"Same as before?" David asked.

"Same as before. The body was packed with money. We recovered a few bills. Our witness says at least twelve people were here, raking the vic for money before everybody took off. That was about 2:45 or so when we got the 9-1-1."

David stared at the face. "Is that?"

"Yep. One Jed Moonstellar. We served a search warrant on this guy and went through the room of Kulis Barney."

"Any idea yet of his last movements?"

"We're checking that now."

Mark David's eyes kept moving across the crime scene, as if making sure he was not leaving something out. He checked his notes. "The woman on the third floor. Did she come down here and touch anything?"

"Naw. Not a chance. She was too scared." Dustin put a gloved hand on his hip. "The techs want us to at least put on a protective mask." David ignored the warning.

Two figures approached them. Chief medical examiner Elly Kent and her assistant Vera Rossin had matching black pants. Each adjusting a facial mask and pulling up gloves. "Can we check him?" Kent asked.

Mark David nodded his okay and the two went through the process of body temp, wound locations and checking for lividity. They worked separately, yet together, with Rossin taking notes as dictated to her from Kent. Thirty minutes later, Kent made an initial report to the two detectives.

"Two to the back of the head. Bullets in the brain, so I'm guessing a small caliber. I'm hoping they weren't removed this time. We think he was brought here, but it's hard to tell with the location so contaminated with people. This happened overnight. And the bills found on him, could be poisoned. This looks exactly like the last victim. Be careful with the bills. We don't know if the killer upped the dosage on the bills. We'll know a lot more later on. I'll have my people take him whenever you are ready."

"Thanks." Mark David finished writing. "No protective wounds?"

"Not a one. My guess is both these guys were comfortable enough with the killer to turn their backs. They didn't expect it." Kent and Rossin wrapped up their gear and left.

The techs were working in full body suits with soft helmets and booties. Almost four hours into the process, the tip of the sun pierced the predawn darkness, branding the horizon with a gold arc, and burned the cloud bottoms red-yellow. More of the sun emerged, bringing the true color of the beach to the naked eye. Mark David turned his back away from the brightness.

Vera Rossin drove back to the scene. She was again running until the sand slowed her down. She reached the detectives huffing big breaths, her bracelet rattling against her wrist. "We're hearing the hospital has two criticals. Both have poison symptoms. And both were here this morning. Looks like we have our worst fears. The money is bad." She didn't wait for a response and turned around, speed-walking to her car.

Mark David was just about to call his office when a uniformed police officer waved to him from the street. By the way he was waving, David knew it had to be important. When he reached the officer, he was pointing to a woman standing next to him. "Sorry to interrupt but she has been here for thirty minutes waiting to talk to you."

When she spoke, the right side of her mouth went up slightly higher than the left. She was animated, using hands and arms to back up her words. "No one will tell me anything."

David's voice sounded calm. "And your name?"

"I'm Lola Henderson. I called the police yesterday and they told me it was too soon."

"Too soon?"

"My boyfriend has been missing since yesterday. We were supposed to meet for dinner and he never showed. I've called him a zillion times and nothing. Goes right to voice mail."

"Who is your boyfriend?"

"Jed Moonstellar."

Mark David motioned for his partner to join him. "You say you were supposed to meet?"

"Yes. We talked in the afternoon just after he got off work from the shop. Business has been light and I was trying to cheer him up. I told him we could go to dinner. On me. It's been one year since we first started dating."

When Dustin arrived, he was briefed on Lola and her connection to Moonstellar. "What made you come out here?" Dustin asked, moving from the sand to the sidewalk.

"I heard about it on the news. I told myself I would not cry, but I wanted to come down here and see for myself."

David posed another question. "You have any details on this person he was supposed to meet?"

"Yes. He was very nervous about it. Scared, I would say. Yeah, he was afraid of this person. Intimidated. The guy was coming to the house. It was supposed to take just a few minutes and then he would come meet me. Just, he never arrived at the restaurant. He met this guy and I never saw him again."

"And who was this person he was meeting?"

# 38

From the start, Mark David knew he was not in control of the situation. The hospital staff directed him to a designated office in the east wing and he was told to stay there and not move. Someone would be with him in a bit. They just didn't know when.

He saw hospital staff moving patients to other areas of the building. In the very short briefing he did get, David was told the hospital was now considered a haz-mat scene. Any new patients were being sent to other hospitals in south Florida, unless they were poison cases. Those cases were now the priority. Three emergency room nurses flashed by him carrying medical supplies. When a door opened, David saw doctors directing people and potential victims on gurneys and they weren't moving.

Paramedics rushed through the doors. On the gurney was a man, David estimated to be around thirty-five years old. He was bleeding from the mouth. A paramedic shouted, "his blood pressure is really low, diarrhea, coughing up blood, not able to speak, and his wife says he's diabetic."

Three emergency room nurses escorted the patient to a room and the doors closed behind them. A security guard ushered people out the door and directed them to the main lobby waiting room. The emergency room, he explained, was now closed to the public. Crowd noise was at a high pitch. People gathered up belongings and complained the entire time.

David took out a pad. He had to think in five different directions and do all of them at the same time. After a few minutes of writing down some quick notes, he jammed his phone to his ear. "It's me. All vacations are cancelled. We work twenty-four seven until we get a handle on this. Yes, I said everyone works. No exceptions."

He waited for some flak on the phone. When he didn't hear any, he kept going. "I need three teams down here at the hospital to talk to doctors and any patients if they let us, to get statements. Got that so far?" He paused. "Good. I need another set of teams to go to each house of every poison patient who was admitted. Get the judges involved. We need warrants now! I want a report ASAP on the money that was found at this newest scene. All of these homes with money need to be crime scenes. I don't care what the mayor says, we're doing a news conference as soon as we get a bit more information. The public has to be warned about this money." He waited until he heard all the proper responses on the phone. "And one last thing. As soon as I clear here, I'm going to pick up Frank Tower. I'm bringing him in." A doctor stood next to him, looking extremely impatient. David ended the call and listened.

"We have a total of seven critical patients. All of them are in various stages of being operated on. We have a lot of tests to do, but I can tell you early on, these all have the same symptoms as Pam Oakman. Their organs are failing and we don't have much time. So far, everyone affected touched that money. This is much worse than before. We are expecting more patients to arrive since we are going by your information that up to a dozen people were at the beach overnight. This is going downhill fast. We are doing what we can and don't expect an update from me for at least two hours. And if you don't leave now, you will be locked in and you won't be permitted to leave until we get a reading on what we have."

"I understand."


Frank Tower heard some vague radio news reports and sized up what he should do. From what he could surmise, people arrived at the rehab center looking for something and realized they were in the wrong place. But why?

He couldn't question the clients on what they saw, and his only source of information came from Jackie.

Other bits and pieces coming from the newscasts gave him one answer. Another body was found. Tower looked out from his window and could not find his police tail. They were obviously too busy to bother watching him. He was just about to leave when a familiar unmarked police unit pulled up. Mark David got out of the car. He looked as grim as a gravestone.

"Been here all night?" David leaned against the car and crossed his arms.

"Yeah. Jackie can vouch for me."

"You sure about that?" David rested his hands on the worn and chipped handcuffs he only wore when he was about to use them.

"Break it down for me, Mark. What's wrong?"

"We found a body on the beach this morning."

"I knew that much. Heard it on the radio."

"The body is Jed Moonstellar."

Mark David waited again, as if weighing the very next flinch from Tower.

"This morning? What's that got to do with me?"

"His girlfriend says you were supposed to meet him. She waited for him but he never showed up. You do anything to him, Frank?"

"I met him at his house. Did a search. And left. That's it. When I took off, he was still alive."

"And you were here all night?"

"Mark, you saw me at 11:30 or so. I was here."

"That gives you plenty of time after I left."

"I promise, it was not me."

"So much for you staying out of the investigation."

Tower's voice let the frustration come through. "You guys are moving too slow. I had to find out more on Kulis. He was staying at Jed's house. I just did some checking. That's it. I've been here, in the back-lot house."

"I've got some bad news."

Tower knew another curveball question was coming. Mark David, his former partner on the force, the man who backed him through a tough money-theft investigation, was about to tell him something with one thing in mind, to get Tower's reaction. A detective thing.

"Like?" Tower stood ready.

"Units just went back to your office. Got a new warrant."

"And?"

"They found a gun. Right there on your desk. Once tests are done, we're convinced it's the nine mil that killed Kulis and Moonstellar."

Tower stood still like one of the faces carved on the side of a mountain. "You and I both know that's not my weapon. I don't own a nine mil."

"I know. You showed us your Glock. We have it. The department thinks you can always have a second piece. Maybe a third. Anything you want to tell me?"

Tower pointed a finger at him. "If you think I'm good for this, arrest me. Right now. We both know someone is setting me up. I stayed here just to stay out of the way. People can vouch for me that I was here. Even your own man."

"We both know you had plenty of time to haul a body down to the beach full of stolen money soaked with poison."

"That's the latest crime scene? It wasn't me."

"I know it doesn't sound like you but everything points your way."

Tower's ease and calm were gone. "Check my stuff. Got nothing to hide. But this bullshit has to stop. I'm guessing there's no prints on that gun. Right?"

"Not so far."

"Right, and you won't find any prints. Someone is going through a lot of work to put me square in the middle. It's not me."

"I know."

"What did you say?" Tower wiped away a bead of sweat.

"What we have on you is circumstantial. The money, the gun. Everything. It doesn't mean anything unless it's tied up."

"But..."

"The but, Frank, is too much is piling up on you. The victim's car was parked near your house. The fingerprints on the money."

"That has to be when I handled the stuff back then."

Mark David looked like he was getting ready to leave, then stopped. "I have to bring you in, even though a good lawyer would tear all this up."

"What about a good detective?" Tower smiled. "How did you get on to the gun?"

"We got a phone call tip. Burner phone with a computer robot voice telling us where to find it."

"Does that sound like your average citizen?"

"No. Everything points to you but it's too easy. You really pissed someone off."

"I'll find out."

A van rolled up and parked. A man and two women got out. Tower recognized them immediately. "Crime techs. For me?"

"They have to gear up, but yes."

The three put on haz-mat gear and protective booties. They approached Tower like he was a piece of evidence. Through the muffled directions through a haz-mat mask, they had Tower hold out his hands. They swabbed his fingers and palms. They also swabbed the front of his pants. Tower saw the door of The Never Too Late open and Jackie marched out like a fullback ready to plow into the line. Tower's expression made her stop and go back inside.

The three-person team retreated to their van. Several minutes later they again bounced out the doors. One person, a woman, walked to Mark David and whispered. The team left.

"You're clean," David said.

"What does that mean? I took a shower?"

"Means they didn't find any trace of the poison on you. And they found nothing at your office."

"Again Mark, I didn't have anything to do with this."

"All I need you to do is come with me, make a statement on where you were overnight, then you're free." Mark David started to open his car door, then stopped.

"No problem. Like I said, I want to cooperate." Tower got in the car. "Sounds like you've got a mess going on."

"I've got search warrants going on at at least seven locations. Patients hanging on to life at the hospital and a news conference in one hour. Beyond that, nothing going on."

The silence became a wall between them. All this was new to Tower. For years, they rode together, keeping these very streets safe. They ran point on search warrants, arrested a team of pickpockets, made dozens of arrests together. Made best cop-of-the-month three times. Now, they were seemingly enemies, with Tower high on a suspect list. The one person who defended him through internal affairs investigations. The two held a bond that was not shaken. Even now.

They crossed over the tracks, leaving T-Town, and drove in the direction of the police station. Tower decided to get bold. "I know you can't share everything, but can I ask, what happened to the evidence found at Moonstellar's' house?"

"You mean our search? You're right, I can't say anything. I was waiting to ask about that at the station."

"Not even about the thumb drive? Was anything on it?"

The car skidded to a stop, with David avoiding a Chevy and pulled his unmarked police car off the road and away from traffic. The jarring hard stop made Tower think the airbags would deploy. Even though the windows were closed, Tower could smell burnt tires.

"What fucking thumb drive?" Mark David shouted.

Tower checked himself and the surroundings. He came close to hitting the dashboard. "Please tell me Moonstellar contacted you."

"No contact. What happened?"

Tower glanced at the door. "Okay if I get out and stretch my legs? This might take awhile. That stop made me think of some felony busts we had."

"So, you hid evidence?"

"He was supposed to call you. I left it all with him. We found the thing in the baseboard. You never got a call?"

"No. And when were you going to tell me?" David gripped the wheel. "His girlfriend said you were supposed to meet him. You know how that looks? The last to see him alive."

"Yes, I met up with him. I instructed Moonstellar to contact you since this was all found at his place?"

"We checked his house."

Tower got out of the car and was hit with the pungent smell of roasted tires. He saw a fifteen-foot long stretch of black rubber on the road. Mark David joined him.

David said, "Okay, I'm calm now. Tell me everything."

## 39

Tower explained everything. He detailed the short visit at the garage, the meet-up at the house, the search of the room where Kulis stayed, the loose baseboard, everything. And he showed Mark the pictures on Tower's phone of the thumbdrive and the note with dates. When he was done, Mark David instructed him to get back in the car. They moved on down the road.

"You weren't supposed to get involved." David talked with his eyes on the road, never looking at Tower.

"I can't clear my own name? I had to do something Mark."

"Did you look at the thumbdrive?"

"No. Like I said, I tried to stay clear of your investigation. I just wanted to make sure you didn't miss anything."

"Looks like I did."

"Sorry Mark. My head's on the chopping block."

"There's one other thing." David was pulling into the police department parking lot. "You were connected to this by Moonstellar's girlfriend. She even had your name."

When they arrived, Tower took a long study of the place where he once worked. "You need to see if she's involved more than just what she's saying."

"Already thought of that. We know where she is and I'll get someone to check her place."

"Warrant?"

"We're in a state of emergency. I'm not waiting for warrants."

Tower's walk into the police building produced the stares one would associate with a zombie stepping into the place. All faces stared at Tower, eyes checking him, then lowered to avoid making eye contact. Mark David escorted him all the way into the detective unit, pointed to a chair and Tower sat, going over memories, some good and some very bad. He looked down the hallway and the room where he strapped up to take a lie detector test on the missing evidence money. Some of the same cash now in evidence again, this time with poison-laced bills.

David was behind a glass-enclosed office. He could see detectives moving about the room like there was a first-tier crisis. The cacophony of police radio conversations echoed in the background. For Tower, the moment was surreal. He once devoted all his working effort to make it into this very room. Be a detective. The money investigation changed all that. After some fifteen minutes, Mark David emerged from the office.

"The forensics team checked your place for chemicals. All rooms in your office, your kitchen. Even went through the garbage, your surveillance van and the garage. They found nothing."

"I could have told you that."

"Haven't even had a drink."

"Not sure what to do with you." Mark David looked like the events of the poisonings were wearing him down, pulling at the mark lines in his face.

Tower offered a suggestion. "Let me go."

"Can't. You're tied too close to this. If you're not a suspect, then you could be a target."

"I can take care of myself."

"Just give me a few hours. Technically, you're free to leave. I can't hold you. But as a..."

"Friend?"

"Former partner, I am asking you to stay here. Just for a bit. I've got some things to go over, then I'll be back."

Tower watched him head back into the glass room, now joined by a cluster of detectives, all with pads out and every so often glancing through the glass at Tower. Up on a large television, a video hookup was in place. They were all talking so loud, Tower could hear everything.

Mark David turned up the volume to the monitor. "Go ahead doctor."

The doctor from the emergency room sounded tired. "We managed to get everyone stable. No loss of life. So far. They are all critical and I'm sorry to say it's going to be a few hours before anyone is able to speak to you. One person kept telling the nurses about the money they were all grabbing up. And no one from the public has been admitted. I'll let you know as soon as they are okay to talk to you."

"Thank you." David turned off the monitor. "What have we got on the video from stores near the beach?"

Detective Dustin turned to Tower. "What's he doing here?"

"I cleared him. Want him where I can see him."

"You cleared him?" The edge in Dustin's voice could cut paper.

"Okay, you have something to hold him on?" David waited for an answer.

A pause turned into a long thirty seconds of nothing from Dustin. Mark David continued. "For the next hour, he stays with me. How are we doing on checking the various homes?"

A tall detective cleared his throat. "We collected, as far as we can tell, close to thirty thousand dollars. All of it is being checked for chemical cont-amination. Lots of folks in haz-mat gear. They have a place a few blocks from here, all closed to the public. They don't want us anywhere near there until they say so. Right now, the early test shows the same type of poison that was used in the first money find. They have not identified the poison, they just know it kills. And no bullets in the body."

"Thanks." David searched the room. "Again, what do we have on surveillance?"

The IT expert checked his notes, almost dropping the pad before he spoke. "There are no cameras in the vicinity of the beach, but we were able to get video of people arriving from a store camera. Too far away for face recognition, but the cars seem to match the ones found at some of the homes. We checked more and the license plates we did get were a match to the homes with the bad money."

David stopped writing. "What about a suspect earlier in the evening?"

"I checked them twice. Will do so again, but I found nothing. I can't explain how that body got to the beach." David posed another question. "These people are being contacted by text message. Do we know where they originated?"

The IT tech rubbed his chin. "We can't locate the original ping location and it has to be from a burner."

Mark David opened a fresh page and continued writing. "If you know, we can move some people on it."

The tech moved in his chair. "Not yet. We think they're coming from a temporary email used to send texts. But it looks like it's bouncing through multiple IP addresses. Right now, we can't trace down the author."

"Thanks." David looked like he was just about to issue assignments.

Medical examiner assistant Vera Rossin stuck her head in the door. "We ran the toxicology reports one more time. We're getting the same result. Something new that is attacking lungs and organs. Wish we had more." She waited as though another question might be coming. "Thanks Vera." Mark David gave a courteous smile. She left.

Frank Tower used his skill of reading lips and the faint words coming from the other side of the glass to determine everything being said in the room. He measured what he was hearing against the bits of information he had already collected. All that was interrupted by the distinct quick clops of six-inch heels on a hard surface.

The woman who approached Tower looked familiar to him. She slowed down her stampede just long enough for a momentary glance at Tower before pushing the door open and entering the meeting room. The door hung open and Tower could hear every word.

"For anyone who doesn't know me, I'm Destiny Row, assistant to the mayor. The chief will be here in a minute. He's been briefed. We need what information you can give for the press conference, which will start in exactly seventeen minutes. What can you tell me?"

Mark David started to speak, only to be cut off by Row. "And could someone please tell me why a first-hand announced suspect in eyes-only emails is sitting out there, calm as an after-sex smoke and not in handcuffs?"

"Because I removed him from the suspect list." Mark David's voice was steady. "Someone has gone through a lot of trouble to push us toward a circumstantial case against Frank Tower. He was not there to do all these things, all backed by alibis. And there is no physical evidence connecting him."

She glared at him the way a person does when faced with a stack of unmatching facts. "You're absolutely sure about this?"

"I'm sure. He's here now only because I want him where everyone can see him. He's not the one we're looking for. I'm positive of that."

Row raised her hand to her hair and placed a loose lock back into position. "I read all your files. Are you doing this because of your years working together?"

"It has nothing to do with that."

"Great," she bellowed. "So, who is the main suspect now?"

There was a great silence in the room. Not even a paper shuffle. For a hot second, Tower's eyes connected with Row's. She turned her attention back to the group. "Fantastic. We've got fifteen minutes now. There's something you should know. The CDC is sending a crew here, although they insist this is still a local case. There is a restaurant ban going into place in one hour, something imposed by the mayor. All restaurants, bars, and most stores will be shut down until we get a handle on this. Grocery stores are considered essential and will stay open, but they no longer accept cash. Only plastic."

Dustin broke in. "These places don't have anything to do with the deaths."

"Public perception," she shot back. "Banks are no longer taking cash. Yes, you heard that right. Banks say they have no way to check the money as customers bring it in. Because of that, they are refusing money. We are about to hit panic mode. No cash. We are in danger of Stilton Bay being shut down. We don't have any other choice. Until you and the people in this room solve this, we're going to see more things closed up and shut down. Tourism going to shit. And you all sit here and tell me the one person we have under suspicion is not the one."

She turned to the door. The heels on a hard floor started up again. When she reached Tower, her expression could freeze a lava flow. She turned back to Mark David and yelled. "Well, come on. We are meeting the media downstairs in the lobby. And bring this former suspect with you."

# 40

One by one, they walked in and sat down at a table. Before them was a collection of microphones, all labeled with TV station numbers. Fifteen feet away a semi-circle of cameras all pointed toward the group like a firing line. Behind each tripod stood a photographer and a reporter. Note pads out, pens ready to write.

"I want to thank you all for being here." Destiny Row's smooth voice exuded confidence. She introduced herself and the members of the group, starting with the police chief Alter, Mark David and a new face to Tower.

"And this is Vera Rossin, who is standing in for the medical examiner."

Tower gave her the PI hard glance. Rossin wore a white coat, hair pulled back, serious and determined. She looked less than eager to be there. A bracelet of natural beads slipped down to her wrist and gave off a hollow sound whenever she moved her hands. The show, however, belonged to Row.

"Please know, we are doing everything we can to find the person or persons responsible for this." Row was direct and polite. "We cannot say anything about the hospitalized victims other than they are stable. We have two homicide victims and information on them right now is part of the investigation. Everything is under control and we are asking the public, if you saw anything on the dates in question, please contact the Stilton Bay police department. I'll take a few questions."

A deep voice from the back spoke up. "We understand you have no suspects. Is that correct?"

Row looked to chief Alter as if waiting for him to speak. When he stayed silent, Row answered. "We are looking in several directions but we need the public's help to find the suspect, yes."

He followed up. "Did you know there is wide-spread panic over this poisoned money? Stores are no longer taking cash; a tour bus went right through the city without making its usual stop. We also understand the car repair shop of the last victim has been closed down, with the owners of four cars inside demanding to get the cars returned."

"We have also heard about these reports." Row again looked to the chief who remained quiet. "We have addressed each one of these situations and we want the public to know Stilton Bay is open for business as usual. We do caution about the money being exchanged."

Vera Rossin spoke up. "The police department has cleared the information I am about to share. The poison is definitely on the money. A contact poison. Please be careful around any money you see. If you start to feel shortness of breath, call 9-1-1 immediately. If you have money that has not been circulated recently, hold on to it. Use your credit cards, debit cards, until we find the source of this tainted money." The bracelet rattled.

Row echoed Rossin's comments. "If you hear talk of having money, cash they got from a crime scene, please let us know. The main thing is people should not panic. Go on with your life. Know that the police department is working hard on this. Go to the beach, go to work. Just be careful of any cash. Thank you for coming."

The three walked out as other questions were shouted, yet no one answered. The huddle of reporters talked among themselves, saying they wanted to ask about the search warrants, how much money was involved, where it came from, and more about the deceased victims. Tower left the room before the reporters turned in his direction. He had all the information he needed, and he knew where he would make his next two stops.

# 41

One main reason Tower liked his office was because the place was the first home he purchased for himself. Modest, with three bedrooms, he considered himself lucky because the zoning was changed to residential/commercial, allowing him to put in a driveway big enough for several cars and turn the place into his office. The thought of someone breaking in and leaving a weapon connected to two murders made him want to spit. Worse, the culprit wanted people to think Tower was the killer. Police had his Glock and the suspect's weapon he had never seen before. Tower went back over the recent events and remembered he turned off the alarm system for the crime techs. The system was never turned back on.

Everywhere he looked, there were traces of where the techs had dusted for prints and evidence. Fortunately, they didn't tear down the door. Tower made sure to give detectives his keys, with hopes they wouldn't destroy the place. Desk drawers were left open, a black film of powder covered the kitchen counter and places on the floor. Tower could tell the filing cabinet had been opened since two drawers were not completely closed. The floor safe under his desk was not touched. Tower opened it and pulled out his backup Glock and holster. He checked to make sure the Glock was in the same condition as when he put it there.

Tower walked to the west wall and adjusted a picture of Shannon Tower until the frame was perfect. The photograph was taken in the Florida Everglades, one of Tower's favorite places. Her eyes matched the sly grin as if she was up to something or had a secret she was going to hold until just the right moment. He blew off the thought of calling her since he promised to leave her alone during her trip. No contact were his last words to her as she left for the airport. She was a good sounding board for his cases and right now, Tower was certain she could give him all sorts of directions on who to trust and how to clear his name. For now, there was just Tower and the investigation.

He looked for where and how the person got inside. All the windows seemed secure. In south Florida, there were no basements, and Tower kept his attention on the windows. In a second inspection, all of them seemed okay.

He sat down.

Normally, Tower would stream some smooth jazz and let the sound bounce around. Today, he just wanted some quiet and to look at everything. The same three holes above the seldom used fireplace were still there, in need of a good spackle job. The fireplace itself was too narrow for anyone to gain access. The office was just like it always was with nothing out of place. A hot beam of light, fueled by the sun, stretched across the floor and would continue to move throughout the day like a laser. He looked for the prism of colors usually found on the other wall. The moment hit him. The colors were in the wrong position. Not by much, but they were off a few inches.

Tower stared at the stained-glass window.

The multi-colored window was about the size of two ice coolers. Tower pulled a ladder from a closet and stepped up. He felt around the edges of the glass and discovered the construction mud around the casing was new. There were no surveillance cameras to confirm this, yet Tower suspected someone carefully chipped around the glass, removed the entire frame and climbed in. Once the gun was planted, the window was sealed up again. Neat job. The only problem was the glass was at a slightly different angle position and that moved the prism of colors. Not much, but enough. Tower took a lot of photographs and decided to wait before sending them to Mark

David until he had more information to share. He continued the survey of his own place.

Outside, just below the stained glass, he found marks on the ground, like the ones from a baseball player's cleats. More photographs. The person who broke in, didn't try to cover up the cleat marks. Tower walked around the office home three more times, yet the search turned up nothing new. When he reached the front door, a woman was waiting for him.

"Sorry to bother you." She had long hair partially hiding hazel eyes and coconut brown skin.

"Can I help you?" Tower tugged on a shoulder harness so his camera was moved to his back.

"I don't know where to start, but I have to ask you a question. Did you kill my boyfriend?"

# 42

On certain words, she raised her left eyebrow, giving Tower the impression she was open in her thoughts, not one to lie. "And your name?" Tower asked.

"Henderson. Lola Henderson. My friends call me Lo." Long fingers tipped in red flashed in front of Tower's eyes as she used her hands when she spoke. "My boyfriend is, was, Jed Moonstellar. We've been going out almost a year now."

"Why do you think I killed him? And more to the point, did you tell the police that?"

"Not in so many words, but you had to be the last one to see him alive."

Tower guided them out of the powerful sunlight until they were now standing in the dappled shadow of a ficus tree in the front yard. "First, I didn't kill Jed. And the last person to see him would have been that person. We did talk, and he showed me the room of a person I was investigating."

She touched her right cheek with one of her crimson-tipped fingers and wiped away any chance of a tear. Both eyes blinked a few times. "I just know I loved him and I was trying to figure out who would kill him and why."

"Did the police say anything about his death?"

"Just that they found him on the beach and he had been shot. They didn't go into any details about the money. Jed was not a big spender. All that business about the money is not him. I don't know where that came from." She was talking fast enough to be considered human speed-dial. Henderson stopped, as if catching herself. She stared into Tower's face. "Can I call you Frank? I know what you're thinking. Did I kill my boyfriend? The answer is no. And I can only think this has to do with that freeloader."

"Kulis Barney?"

"Yeah, him. He arrived, didn't work, didn't do anything."

"You meet him?"

"Just once. He stayed in that back room. It was creepy. He kept opening the door and trying to listen to our conversations. Weirded me out."

"Why did Jed let him stay there?"

"I can't imagine why. All I know is he was so secretive. I didn't like it. Like he was hiding something. One time he came out of the room and I could see he had been on his laptop. As soon as I looked that way, he went back and closed the door."

"Any idea why he came here?"

"Just that Jed said he was going to make things right. I don't know what that means." Again, the eyes bored into Tower. "I know you didn't kill Jed. I've studied all the news reports. It's sad about all those poisonings. But I have to ask you a question."

"Yes."

"I want to hire you. To protect me and find out who killed him."

"The police are working on that."

"They're too busy trying to calm the panic. I need another set of eyes. Yours, Mr. Tower."

"You sure you want to do that? You just asked me if I killed him."

"I'm positive. The other day a van drove by my place and stayed awhile, just watching my front door."

"You see the driver? Get any plates?"

"No to both questions. The van drove off when I opened my door. But I'm scared. Maybe they think Jed told me something."

"You tell the police?"

"Not yet."

For Tower's five-year span as a PI, taking on a new client centered on a lot of facts, including the B.S. factor. He had to figure in a short time if she was truthful. The ability to pay was another, but in this case, he was more than curious. He had a vested, purely personal reason to find out what she knew regarding the two dead men.

"I'll take you on as a client, but you have to share this information with Detective Mark David, is that clear?"

"Clear. What now?"

"We'll go into the office. Give me some information I need and I'll start your case."

"Thank you."

# 43

Detective Mark David was only going to stop in his office for just a hot second. There was too much to do. A knock on the door stopped him from leaving.

"I know you're busy, but I just wanted a word." The word was coming from the mayor of Stilton Bay. Vernon Thomas was much taller than on television. "I'll just stand because I won't be long." His cuffs bore his initials, the heavy starched collar looked to be double thickness. He unbuttoned the suit, revealing a silk red tie. "I want to make this real clear, no matter what Destiny Row tells you. I want your team to do whatever is needed and say whatever you need to say to find this person."

"Thank you, mayor." Mark David tucked a few papers along with his pad and jammed them under his arm. "I was there when they named a street after you. This whole town is on nerves, I know."

"This guy Frank Tower. Can he really help you?"

"As you know, he's no longer on the force. And while I can't talk about it, he was on our radar for being involved in this."

"I know Frank. And beyond that, I remember the troubles his mother went through. Jackie. Glad to see she's doing better." He paused. "We're getting some national attention because of the dirty money. And tourism is off. To be honest, off a lot. But I don't wan't you to worry about that. Is that clear?"

"Should I call the chief in here?"

"No. He knows I'm here. I must tell you I've been fielding calls for the FBI to come in here and piledrive their way around on this case, but I'm not letting that happen. My confidence is in you and your people."

"Thank you." David moved closer to him as if to leave the room. "I like the confidence you're giving me, but there is something you're not saying. Isn't there?"

"There is, I can't lie about that. While there is no call for federal authorities now, there is some pressure on me for a deadline."

"Deadline?"

"Maybe that's the wrong word. What about needed assistance. I spoke to the chief about it, and he's onboard with the thinking."

"And what thinking is that? Mayor, just what is needed assistance?"

"We need to wrap this up. And if that means we bring in some additional help at some point, some needed assistance, I'm all for it."

"Well mayor, isn't that like pressure?"

"I don't see it that way. We're all trying to solve this, aren't we? This is just something down the road, so to speak, that will give us some help."

"And by help, what do you mean?"

"I'm really not sure right now. Just know, we're ready to step in and help."

"Quite frankly, sir, any new help right now would just slow us down. I have no idea what you mean by bringing in more people, but my department will get this done. And down the road, as you say, if the case needs it, I might even bring in Frank Tower to help."

"Sounds good to me." Thomas made no sounds as he left the office, almost as if he was never there.

## 44

Lucas Park smiled at the chaos. On the drive to the hospital, he saw long lines building at gas stations where attendants refused to take cash. People were starting to hoard everything from gasoline, water, toilet paper, to just about anything a person would touch. He passed closed restaurants. Many others were headed north on the Florida Turnpike out of Stilton Bay. There were false rumors. Reporters whack-a-moled each fictitious story about the quality of the drinking water, that it was not tainted. All because of the poison-laden money found on two bodies.

Park loved chaos.

A driver cut him off and almost stole the parking space. Park instead stepped on the gas and aimed his own car to ram into the space thief. The other car moved off. Again, Park smiled. The conditions were perfect for him. Armed security watched the entrance and Park was only allowed to enter because of his connection to a patient. People, thinking they had touched money that would harm them, were sent to other locations for testing. In watching the news, he saw more than five interviews with supposed witnesses who gave the wrong information about the money and the poison. Park knew the real facts, he was there. All the bad information served his purposes. People didn't know what to believe. Just what Park wanted.

Chaos.

Just what Lucas Park needed to slip into his wife's room and cause her death.

He flashed a driver's license and walked through a metal detector before heading to the elevator. Down the hallway, several doctors and nurses crisscrossed in front of him. Tiny bits of conversation about recovery efforts on poison patients bounced off the walls. The visitor pass stuck to Park's shirt gave him permission to move about undeterred. Once off the elevator, a simple smile to the one person at the nursing station and Park was free to enter Joni's room.

The two police officers normally guarding her door were gone. Must be the chaos, he thought.

Park opened the door to the sounds of a ventilator helping Joni Park stay alive. Other machines monitored her blood pressure and heart rate. She was connected to a series of clear tubes pumping liquids into her body. For a few minutes, Park just sat there, wondering if he should disconnect anything. He tried to be quiet. Park whispered a dammit, aimed at himself for not sneaking something into the hospital to carry out his plan. If he unplugged anything, he reasoned, the nurses would get word rather fast and come running into the room. After weighing all his options, Park walked to a closet and eased a pillow from the shelf.

He walked zombie-like holding the pillow and moved in the direction of his sleeping wife. In her coma, she looked as if she was already in the grip of death. Her chest barely raising, hands and fingers never moving, every muscle fixed in place. Park heard each of his own steps as he approached her. For some reason, the pillow felt heavy. He stopped at her bedside and kept the pillow next to her face. Next would be a two-step move. First, he had to ease the pillow over her, then ease it directly over her face then pushing down for as long as needed.

Lucas paused as he held the pillow inches from her nose and mouth. Memories, good and bad, swept over him like a strong current. The first few years were livable, followed by more than a decade of taunts, since he couldn't find work, never finished college, and kept almost no friends. For him, confidence was an elixir he never got to taste. Each day was misery until he started working on loosening the balcony. Park looked over his shoulder one more time. He listened for any footsteps in the hallway and lowered the pillow until it almost touched her skin.

Adrenalin shot through his body like a junkie absorbing heroin. He kept a half-smile smirk on his face so long, a ball of drool formed at the corners of his lips. An avalanche of thoughts pounded his brain that he was actually going through with killing her. There was no compulsion to stop or weigh the gravity of what was about to take place. Park just wanted to complete the deed. He dreamt about a moment like this one. Euphoria replaced the fear of being caught. Park aimed the pillow to cover her entire face, hoping to take away her last few breaths of air.

Park shouted, "die bitch!"

His shout must have done something. He looked down to see movement in her fingers. Park put the pillow to the side.

For the first time since the poison gripped her body, Joni Park opened her eyes.

# 45

On his way home from the hospital, Park wanted to shrink inside his clothes. He failed in his mission. Instead of achieving his goal, he received accolades and a pat on the back from the doctor for doing something, anything to wake up the sleeping Joni Park. He pounded the steering wheel, causing the horn to sound each time.

Everything was in place. He had beefed up her insurance policy years earlier to hopefully stifle any suspicion from police, showing nothing was done recently. The two words kept coming at him like body-seeking arrows. Die bitch!

Every so often he checked his phone to see if there was another anonymous text. One that would lead to another big stash of cash. Park kept glancing at the phone like a hooker looking for the next john.

He was informed Joni was still very groggy and probably wouldn't be able to speak for several days, maybe weeks. The whole situation just added to his worry list. What if she talked to a nurse about the money? Once detectives got word she was awake, how long before they came asking more damn questions. Lucas grinned.

Chaos.

Lucas surmised they would be too busy tracking the killer of the two victims, they wouldn't have time to come back to Joni. The events unfolding in Stilton Bay were now national news. They don't have time for her, he thought. His car drive did not take him back to his apartment. Yes, the railing on his balcony was so loose now, just a cough of the Florida wind would send the thing over and down several flights. He just had to get her back out there and let her stand in her usual place to observe the view. All he had to do was find a way to entice her.

For now, he was somewhere else. He had no reason to come this way. Lucas parked and watched the building. All of his attention centered on the door, watching each person who came and left. He had no place to go. This was now his new mission. Just wait. The constant checks of the watch would have to stop. He didn't know the plan. He only knew he had to wait. He sat there, hands gripping the wheel.

Now he just wanted to see the face of Cason Willow.

# 46

Tower let him examine the photographs on his cell phone. The man studied them for several minutes, then handed the phone back to Tower.

"I think you're right, but it's hard to tell. That mark could have been made by anything." Ray Syth was wiry. The tops of his hands were scratched and calloused. His speckled gray hair was left uncombed and the flannel shirt was untucked. "I've sold all kinds of gear to climbers for going on ten years. But yeah, this could have been made by crampons."

"Crampons?" Tower asked.

"Metal cleats going over hiking boots or snow boots to go up and over ice or snow. Believe it not, I sell a lot of them here in Florida."

"I believe you." Tower looked at the wall of climbing gear.

"I'm in my last few months." Syth looked like a man down to his last quarter. "Online stores have wiped me out. They don't need to come in and try on anything anymore. Just click and spend."

"Sorry to hear that." Tower was almost finished. "Anyone come in to buy cleats. Recently, or in the past couple of years?"

"Naw, nothing I can remember. How high up did you see the marks?"

"The window that was removed is up a bit since my building has high vaulted ceilings. So, you're talking about twenty feet."

"That would be nothing for a climber. You see any anchor marks?"

"Outside, I have an exposed beam. Easy for anyone to toss a climber's rope and scale the wall."

"Hope you find him."

Tower moved for the door. "Thanks for your help."

## 47

Lucas Park waited until Cason Willow stepped outside the apartment complex and moved toward him. When he touched his shoulder, Willow jumped.

"What do you want?" Willow grunted.

"I need your help," Park said.

"Whatever you are planning, I am done. Ya hear me? Done. My girl-friend never wanted me to be a part of this."

"You mean you don't want in on the next text? You know it's gonna come. Together, we can haul in a lot more than anyone else."

"The only thing I want is to distance myself from all of this. You watching the news? This thing is killing people. It's not worth the risk."

Park reached in his pocket and held his cell phone at his side. "I need you with me just one more time. One last score. We join up to do the haul."

"I don't think you've been listening to me." Willow pointed a finger at Park, jabbing at the air with each word. "I am done. Through. Get someone else."

Park remained composed, his voice level. There was no malice in his tone, just the unfrenzied calm of a someone about to make a point. "Look at the picture on my phone Cason. That's you." Park held up the phone like a weapon. "Yea, during all that mess, I took the time to photograph you, raking in the cash. Proof that you were there, stealing that money."

"You were there! I was the one who wanted to call police."

Park yelled, "You took the money. What if this picture got into the hands of police? What if someone told them you planned the meet-up? That it was you who took most of the most cash."

"That was on you. You were angry you couldn't get more."

Park smiled. "Naw, that's not what the police will hear. They will be told you fought off everyone else for the money, that you ripped those bills from the chest of a dead man to feed your own greed. We just followed your lead."

"I took the least amount. I'm sure of it."

Park tucked the phone away. "The police will think you spent most of the money. You'll go away to prison for ten years."

"I'll tell them it was you." Willow shouted, then looked around as if people could hear him and lowered his voice. "I'll explain everything. That you wanted more money. Couldn't get enough. Just you!"

"I'll tell them I found that money. And my wife touched the stuff and got sick. They already feel sorry for me. Who do you think they'll believe? You have one choice, Cason. Help me with the next stash. I want all the money you get or I'll make you the lead story on the news. Now, which will it be?"

## 48

Lola Henderson got out of her car. She stepped toward the townhouse and found the parking lot unusually quiet. The birds and cicadas stopped their night songs and the tree limbs drooped in the humidity. Lola felt alone. The front door to her place was a good two-hundred feet away. Without designated parking spaces and the last to arrive, she was forced to get a spot a good distance away. The one-time picturesque foliage now resembled hiding places and attack points for someone with evil intentions. Lola reached for her phone, dropping the thing in the process. The clatter echoed off the darkened windows of her neighbor's homes. The phone was cracked yet maybe it would still work. Maybe.

Just as she started to quicken her pace, she heard something behind her. Lola's head whipped around toward her car expecting a friendly face, only to see a long line of tree shadows.

There was the sound again. Possibly a hard foot on the ground. "Who's there?" she said to the tall palms. Lola was supposed to turn and run. Get to her door as soon as she could, try the cell phone. Call Frank Tower. Yet, all she could do was stand there, frozen in the Florida heat, waiting to be picked off like some target in a carnival shooting gallery. Her breathing was haphazard and she felt herself trembling. "If someone is there, I'm about to call the police."

Nothing.

Her closest option was her car. Lola started searching her purse for the keys to the BMW, and stopped. One glance and fear crept over her. The car keys were on the front seat of the driver's side. She moved to the car, and tried the handle only to find the door was locked. Keys inside. Again, the silence took over. The sky was a mat of black with only a thin sliver of moon, carved like a razor cut. She walked two paces. Then three more. She stopped. Lola was convinced she saw something.

For a moment, she made out the distinct form of a person's shadow moving left to right behind her. She turned and saw only her car, bathed by a single streetlight.

Lola ran.

Her motion resulted in a loud bouncing collection of everything in her purse and the thumps on pavement from shoes never intended for wind sprints. In her range of vision, all objects were moving around with her herky-jerky running style. Her last attempt at a good run had been eleven years ago while being chased by a former college boyfriend. Tentacles of pain reached up into her thighs as she quickly used up the muscle glycogen in her legs. Her lungs were empty sacks. She made it to the door and was thankful her house keys were on a different ring than the car fob. Twice she dropped the keys, finally getting inside on the third try. She kept the lights off and parted a blind, checking the street for anyone following her. Her breathing was a series of deep panting. The next task was to calm down. Lola grabbed her phone and dialed Frank Tower.

He answered on the first ring. "You have to make it quick. What's up?"

"Someone..." She could only get out the one word, given the limited air supply. "Someone was out there." Lola took thirty seconds to say a few words. Her body, lungs, everything, were depleted from the run.

"Where are you? You okay?"

"I'm home."

"You see anyone?"

"No, I don't think so. I thought someone was following me."

"You're in the house?"

"Yeah...I ran."

"Stay inside. I'm on my way, but you have to go with me."

"Go? Where?"

Tower took a moment before he answered. "Someone from the department, Detective Sam Dustin is missing."

## 49

Frank Tower saw Lola's tired eyes and made the suggestion for the fourth time. "Why don't you sleep? I'll wake you up when we get to the station."

"I can't sleep." She looked at the houses slipping by as they drove. "Thanks for coming. My spare car key was in the bedroom."

"No problem." Tower said. "I did find some tire tracks like someone took off in a hurry. And a dented portion of a hedge. Maybe someone was there."

"Someone was there. I know it!" She rubbed her eyes.

"Did Jed ever talk to you about the thumbdrive?"

"Someone was there. I know it!" She rubbed her eyes.

"Did Jed ever talk about a thumbdrive?"

"No, it never came up."

Tower said, "I had a concern that the wrong person might think you had the drive and would come after you."

She shrugged. "That's comforting. You sayn' I'm in danger?"

Tower didn't answer right away. "And I'm concerned whoever killed your boyfriend and the first victim might be holding Sam. If we don't act fast, he could be the next victim."

"Jed didn't have to die that way." She leaned her head on the passenger side window.

"If they're desperate, maybe they think Sam has the drive?" Tower kicked up the speed. "If the killer knows the police do not have the thumb-drive, they have to think you have it or someone else. Can you think of where Jed might hide it?"

"Not really. Let me think about it."

Tower turned into a section of T-Town. "That also crossed my mind." Gone were the pristine street lights bought by the city council.

"Wow. Look at them. It's two A.M." Lola's left eyebrow moved upward. She counted at least six prostitutes lining the block. Each with her own exotic style of clothing, or lack of clothes. As Tower passed, all of them tried to lock eye contact with her.

"Sorry I had to take you this way. It's a shortcut to the police station. Meet the women of T-Town." Four of them waved to Tower.

"They know you."

"Yeah, the ones I arrested know me. The rest are too young. I've been gone five years."

"You grow up around here?" Lola's eyes were fixed on the moldy-gray houses.

"Yes." He glanced at a shuttered house, then back on the road. "T-Town doesn't get much help." The area was on the west side of Stilton Bay, away from the tourist buses and the five-star restaurants. Away from the ocean, away from the city revitalization plan and visits from the mayor unless there was an election. T-Town was a worn blight on the town like a blister that never heals. Four lamp posts were burned out, giving the street a partial lighted way. A tiny convenience store was still open; dim inside, yet Lola could see the rows of booze bottles lining the shelves.

"Lots of robberies right there," Tower said. "Made a lot of stops when I was on the street. Don't miss it." He pointed down the block. "See down there? That apartment building?"

Lola nodded.

"They once found me wandering the street here with just a shirt and dirty underwear. I was three at the time."

"Where was your mother?"

"Good question. She had this thing for drugs and leaving me to get more. The people here sorta raised me. I made it somehow."

Tower's thoughts were a mix of his childhood and the case. He let his mind wander again to the street for just a moment. With so much attention on the tainted money, police stops in T-Town would be down to a minimum. Drug deals were probably going unchecked. A tall woman, wearing black fishnet stockings, a tube top and a purple wig wagged a finger at them, motioning for Tower to pull over. The woman grinned and pretended she was about to lift the top. Then stopped.

"Where are..."

"Their customers? We're close to I-95. The Johns drop off the expressway, come into T-Town, get their johnsons drained and head back on out of town. Sorry to be so blunt."

They passed the Never Too Late drug rehabilitation center, yet Tower didn't say anything about the place or Jackie. They left T-Town and emerged at the north end of the city. When they got out of the car, the place was active. Every light was on in the building. Police cars coming and going.

Mark David met them in the parking lot. "Thanks for coming Frank." He handed Tower a piece of paper. "With this bad money and two homicides, my people are stretched thin and tired. If anyone gives you any shit, show them this paper. Signed by the Mayor and the chief. You are now a special consultant to the police department. Just please, if you think you have something, call me right away. Don't move in. Backup. And whatever you do, don't shoot anyone."

"Don't plan on it. What do you need me to do?"

"We're processing Sam's unmarked. The car was parked just outside his house. His gun, badge and cell phone were left on the front seat. Wife home. She didn't hear or see anything. There was a slight smell of something telling us he was drugged. It had to be someone he knew. He'd never be taken like that without a fight. I texted you three locations we need checked. These are the last known places Sam went. Just see if anyone can give us a sighting. Some information. Anything. Maybe surveillance video." David turned to Lola. "Sorry about your boyfriend. We're doing everything we can."

"I know."

Tower pulled Mark David away from Lola. "When Jed disappeared, we found his body twenty-four hours later. That was probably the same timetable for Kulis Barney."

"I know what you're saying Frank. The clock is ticking. If Sam was really taken, then we don't have much time."

"One last thing. Anything new on the missing thumbdrive?"

"Not yet. But it just dropped on my list."

Tower nodded. "Understood."


Tower and Lola returned to his car. Tower stopped. A blue vehicle, engine revved up, turned the corner of the building, zoomed past them and kept going. Now it was Tower's turn to run. His pace was quick, and he concentrated his sight on the back seat of the blue car rather than a license plate. Now with a pair of sneakers instead of heels, Lola was close behind him.

"What's the deal with that car?" Her eyes were fixed on the side road next to the station.

"Maybe there's a surveillance camera for back here," Tower thought out loud. "The back seat of that car had climbing gear."

# 50

Tower searched his cell phone directory while he drove, then opted to pull over. He looked through the names on his contact list. He touched a number and waited.

"Stilton Bay police..." The voice was coming through so loud, Tower didn't need to put it on speaker phone.

"It's Frank. Frank Tower." Tower didn't give him a chance to hang up. "Listen, you probably heard I'm consulting for the department and I need a favor."

"Does Mark know about this?"

"He's busy doing a ton of things and we have to move fast on a lot of angles, you with me?"

"Yeah. I'm not so sure about this, but what do you need?"

"You have a surveillance camera or two on the East side of the station?"

"We've got three."

"Great. When you have a free moment, and I know that's tough right now, look for a car exactly around seven minutes ago. A blue car. It should have some type of mountain climbing gear in the back. I need a video sample."

"I don't know Frank."

"How long have I worked with you?"

"Lately?"

"You know what I mean. Didn't I come through for you when you lost two hours of video in that purse theft ring?"

"We don't have to get into that right now." The voice paused. "Okay, Frank. I'll look for it. Please tell me this is related to this case. We're all in shock over Sam."

"It has everything to do with the case. Whatever you can give me."

"If Mark finds out about this, he'll have my ass."

"He won't. Thanks. How long will it take?"

"Well, I've got two projects first, then I'll get to it."

"Thanks again."

"Who was that?" Lola was transfixed on Tower.

"Someone I know in the department. Just a hunch."


Sixteen minutes later, Tower and Lola were in front of a car parts store. Tower turned to Lola. "I'll leave the engine running. Listen, I know the police checked Jed's house and garage. Would there be another property that he owns? I checked the county records and only found the two locations. Home and his business."

Lola looked out through the front windshield, parting her hair, then repeating the whole process again. "The only thing I can think of is his rental place."

"Here in Stilton Bay?"

"Yes. Been there once. Creepy place. He didn't believe in cleaning up much. He never gave up the lease. Keeps saying he's going to fix it up. Never did."

"Thanks. I'll be right back."

Tower walked into the shop. There was a slight smell of engine oil. A black woman walked to the front, emerging from two tall shelf cases full of car parts. She looked at Tower from his shoes to his hair and frowned. "Whatever it is, I don't need it or I already have it."

"Hi. The name's Frank Tower. I'm working with the Stilton Bay Police Department. You have a minute?"

"Not really, but go ahead." Her eyebrows converged.

"I'm here checking. Did you speak with a Detective Sam Dustin the other day? Big guy, kinda gruff?"

"The guy who never smiled? Yeah, I 'member him."

"Did anyone else come in behind him, asking questions?"

"You mean, like you? Naw, just him. What, he forgot to ask me something? He asked about one of my regulars. Jed. Really sad what happened to him."

"Yes, Jed. When Jed or Sam left, did anyone follow them, if you know?"

"Honey, I'm so busy in here, I don't have time to check out people all the way out to their cars."

"What about cameras?"

"Yeah, I got a few. It's here in the back."

Tower followed her to a back office, near the public restroom. Three camera pictures were being fed to monitors. Tower saw his car in the parking lot and Lola looking bored.

"Can you cue up Sam's visit?" He wanted to see Jed's video as well, but Sam was the priority. She sat down to a computer covered in a thick layer of store dust. In three minutes, she stopped.

"Here you go."

Tower found Sam on one camera talking to the store owner until he walked out. Another camera showed him going to his car, stopping for a moment to check his phone, then driving off. Everything looked normal until Sam's car drove off out of sight. The angle was poor, but Tower saw the outline of the car he had seen in the police station parking lot. The driver was not recognizable.

"Burn me a copy of this, if you could. That would be great."

"Always like to help when I can."

"Not now, but I'd like a copy of Jed's recent visits. I'll come back to pick them up. That okay?"

"Sure."

Tower walked to the car. His phone rang. "Tower..."

"It's me. Your old friend on the IT cameras. That task you had me do, I finished."

"And?"

"It's nothing. No big deal. Dead end. She's in here all the time."

"Who?"

"The medical examiner, Elly Kent."

# 51

Mark David's fist came down so hard on his desk, Tower thought the office door would rattle. "You don't go over my head, Frank!"

"You were busy."

"We've got everyone out, checking every possible lead and you tie up my IT tech with a search that leads us to the medical examiner. Elly would have your head if she found out."

"I know you two are close. I didn't know it was her car. We didn't get a plate but a car similar to hers was spotted. Twice."

"C'mon, Frank! Spotted in our parking lot, where she comes and goes all the time. And maybe, I repeat maybe at a car parts store. That isn't evidence Frank, it's a waste of time. We have no clue on where to find Sam, and this is a complete dead end."

Tower thought about what he would say next. Elly and Mark dated for almost a year; they were still very close friends after the breakup. Just hours working with the department and already Tower was the subject and target of a shouting session. Tower's suggestion came in a low tone. "If it's okay with you, just let me do one thing. It won't take long, I promise."

"Please don't tell me you plan on approaching Elly with this bullshit?"

"No, nothing like that. I just want to check something out. And once that's done, I'll leave it alone."

"This stays between us. Go do your hunch and get back to me. Just me, understand?"

"No problem."

Tower marched out of the office, determined to find an answer behind the blue car. He went outside, where Lola was waiting for him. He dialed a number for the first time in five years. He waited. "JoJo? It's Frank. You got a minute?" For the next six minutes Tower spoke to JoJo Hardaway, a federal agent. An old friend. He finished by mentioning several photographs and pieces of video, before sending them to JoJo. "How soon can you get back to me? We have to find Sam soon."

"Give me an hour," She said.

Tower met JoJo at a gas station. Lola was asleep in the car. Tower hadn't slept for a solid twenty hours. A Florida sunrise burned a yellow hue into the sidewalks and buildings. JoJo Hardaway pulled up in a faded green Honda with three dents in the side. She got out and her usual smile was absent. "Hi Frank."

She moved into the shade and studied Tower. "You need to mainline some coffee."

"I know. Been up all night. We got to find our detective."

"I want to thank you."

"Why?"

She looked around as if to check who might be listening. "We ran all your photographs and video through face rec, just for giggles. Now, this is just between you, me and the D.E.A. For now, it can't go anywhere else."

"You know me, JoJo. I wouldn't say anything."

"Part of what I'm about to tell you, I'll let you pass on to Mark. But this could turn out to be one dogshit mess. Ya got me, Frank?"

"Sure." Tower stepped a bit closer, curiosity taking him over.

"When the pictures went through our checks, we noticed something. I should say, someone. This person has been on our radar for a long time and if it's who we think it is, we haven't seen her in years. My badge would get a free buffing if I could bring her in."

"JoJo, you're killing me. Who is it? What did you find on Elly Kent. She tied up with some crime thugs, or what?"

"It's not Elly Kent. She's clean, far as we're concerned. No Frank, the person we want is standing next to her in the first photograph you sent me."

# 52

Tower's driving woke up Lola. "Damn Frank, where's the fire?"

The car almost hit a Volvo moving through the intersection. Tower ignored the red light and stepped harder on the gas pedal. He dialed while he was driving. "Where's Mark David?"

The voice on the other end was faint. "He's not here."

"Get him. Tell him Frank Tower says it's urgent! I've got to see him as soon as possible."

"I can get another detective..."

"No! Just Mark. It's more than urgent. Tell him to meet me at Elly Kent's office. You get that? Elly Kent." Tower ended the call before he could answer. A car door started to open in front of him. Tower swerved a bit, just missing the door and forcing the driver back inside to avoid being hit.

"Frank, what is going on?" Lola asked.

"I can't tell you just yet. When we get to this location, I want you to find someplace safe. Is that clear?"

"Why? I thought you said..."

"Get yourself to a safe place. Just do that for me."

. . .

Twelve minutes later, Tower parked his car and gave the fob to Lola. "If you think anything is not right, get out of here."

"Where are you going?"

"Inside that building. Not sure what's going to happen but get ready to leave if you hear or see anything out of the ordinary."

Mark David parked next to Tower. He stepped hard on the pavement. "This better be worth my time. We're hoping the guy holding Sam will call with a ransom."

"Follow my lead. We're first looking for Elly."

Mark David flashed a badge once inside the lobby of the medical examiner's office. He moved past the secretary without a wave or acknowledgement and went directly into her office. Elly looked up, startled.

"Mark, something wrong?"

"Tower has something to say."

Frank directed Elly to her computer. "Is all of your staff here?"

"No, I don't think so. We don't have anything scheduled, so I gave a few people the day off."

He handed her a piece of paper. "Go to this website. It's a database. And type in the name."

"Okay." She typed in the website, waited and before entering the name she stopped. "Why, this is-"

Tower said, "We know. Just type in the name."

Elly typed the name and waited. A photograph and a bio appeared on the computer screen. "Who is this?"

Tower stepped closer to the computer. "Your assistant, what's her name?"

A look of concern etched Elly's face. "Vera Rossin."

Tower tapped the screen. "Meet the real Vera Rossin. She died six years ago."

# 53

Elly Kent propped up her head with her hand and stared into the computer. Her voice crackled with anger. "We all vetted her. We checked her out. Well, who is she?" She turned to the two men standing next to her.

Tower started. "Her real name is Peona Wren. She is a rogue D.E.A. informant. When they last tracked her, she dropped off their radar four years ago when she failed to check in with her handler. They have been looking for her ever since. She was busted for running a meth lab and was well-known for her ability to mix chemicals."

Mark David spoke up, "I'll make the call to the chief to roll SWAT to her apartment. We can join them there."

"She was right under my nose!" Kent yelled to the wall.

"She had all of us fooled. Remember, she was the one who gave us the tip about the text message." Mark David tried to comfort her. He checked his watch. "We don't have much time. It gets worse."

"Worse?" Fear crept into her eyes.

"From what I know about her, she's a master at forging documents. I was sent a redacted file on her, which I'll pass on to you. Two other things. But I have to ask you, was she using your car?" Tower asked.

"Yes. I had her running some errands, running around town. I didn't think there would be a problem. But she returned it."

Tower followed up. "The ropes and climbing gear in the car. Are they yours?"

"No. She asked if she could store them just for a few days. She got them out this morning. You said, it's worse?"

Tower grabbed his own wrist. "I noticed she kept fiddling with a bracelet during the news conference. Or when I saw her last."

"Yes..."

"Well, we froze that picture and examined, as best we could, the bracelet. And it looks to us that the bracelet is made up of castor beans."

Kent's voice rose an octave. "Castor beans, as in deadly ricin?"

Tower answered, "The same. Now, just wearing those beans can be a problem. As you know, what we're dealing with here on our money is some form of that, but not ricin. We've never seen it before. So, it looks like she was capable of making this or having someone help her prepare the poison to put on the money."

Tower said, "About the money." Mark David started moving to the door until Tower stopped him. "We already knew a lot of the money came from the heist of cash that was headed to the evidence room. That money we knew about. That is separate. What we are finding out from the D.E.A. is that while she was working as an informant, Wren was in the pipeline for drug money going back to its source. Wren, we are told, stole a large shipment of money that was headed out of the United States. Drug money. Money she was moving for years and then, finally as an informant. Well, a large amount of the stolen money was marked and in the process of being tracked. She, along with the feds knew about the tracking. What we're saying is that most of the cash stuffed into the clothing of our two victims, is money stolen from the drug cartel."

Kent hissed. "The cartel?"

David opened the door to leave. "By now, the cartel hunted her down and they know where their money is and that it's in the hands of everyone who grabbed money off those bodies. And everyone else in Stilton Bay who unknowingly got some of that money."

Tower joined him at the door to leave. "And the cartel is not going to be happy about it. The whole town is at risk of reprisal."

# 54

A line of twelve Stilton Bay police officers lined up against a wall and in the shade. All veteran members of the SWAT unit, they were armed with semi-automatic rifles, shot guns, helmets, armor chest plates, knee pads and their service weapons. Two other officers, pretending to be a couple shopping, went door-to-door, getting people out and away from any potential danger. Once the floors were cleared of any civilians, they could move in. Across the street, on the roof of two buildings, snipers were prone in position, a bolt action rifle aimed and ready.

Tower was two cars behind Mark David. Next to Tower was a very groggy Lola. "What are they doing, lined up like that?" She asked.

"It's called the snake. "They're in a row like that to make themselves as little of a target as possible." He pointed to the officer in front, a tall woman wearing black gloves. "The officer in front is the point. Once they gain entry, they will take positions, something they've already discussed. Each person will take an area." Tower rubbed his tired eyes.

There was always a stillness just before the snake moved on a strike. An early morning sun bored in on the windows of the apartments. An advantage for the snake. Anyone looking outside would have to squint. Blinds for Vera Rossin's apartment were closed. The point team member moved and the snake moved with her. They stopped.

A block away, Tower could barely make out the gathering of people escorted out of the building. He was too far away to see, yet Tower knew there would be anxious faces with questions the police would not answer yet. The take-down took longer to organize as the building across the street was difficult to empty. Four places he was told had parents with children. Moving kids always takes time. Then, building managers had to be found, keys obtained to get access to the roof. They were out of sight, but Tower knew snipers were in position. All attention now was on the snake.

Guns raised, the twelve moved in a well-organized manner, quiet and quick. They reached the second-floor apartment. And paused.

"You want to be with them, don't you?" Lola was watching Tower.

"Maybe."

"I can tell."

Tower's eyes never moved from the apartment. "That was a hundred years ago."

A loud noise was followed by the door busting off its hinges. The snake had entered and was inside. Everyone on the ground waited, as if expecting a shot. Twenty seconds turned into ninety seconds. Then four minutes. Tower was positive he heard an all clear. The point came out and raised her hand for Mark David to come upstairs. He moved up the stairs two at a time. Once inside, there was another wait. A good ten minutes. When Mark David emerged from the apartment, he motioned for Tower to join him.

When Tower reached apartment 201, he was cautioned to stay at the door and not enter. "She's not here and there's no sign so far of Sam. But I wanted you to see this." He pointed to a far wall.

"We removed a painting and found this." Mark David made sure Tower did not enter the apartment. On the far wall, there were several pictures of Tower, all shot in surveillance-mode, in black and white, from the street level. Photographs of Tower at a restaurant, coming out of a gym, and one in front of his office house. "Looks like she's been watching you for some time." Mark David allowed Tower to step onto a square, placed there by the officers who all filed out and went downstairs. "Frank, I'm letting you inside because you were a target. Could still be one."

Tower looked around the room. The place was a one-bedroom affair and he could see the scrambled mess of blankets from the unmade bed. Off to his right was a small kitchen. Dirty dishes were piled high in the sink. On his left, a desk and the huge arrangement of pictures. There was a laptop with a screensaver with Tower's face. "She really has a thing for you," David said, making sure his gloves were on tight.

"Since I can't go anywhere," Tower stared, "Can you tap the laptop and see if it's on?"

Mark David touched the screen. The computer was not in a lockdown mode. Anyone could access the files that popped up on the monitor.

"She wants us to see this." Tower pointed to the computer.

The detective scrolled around. "We don't see any evidence of Sam, but there's got to be something in the computer files." He opened a file and started at video of Vera with a backpack on, hiking boots and a floppy hat. The backpack was no ordinary setup.

"That's how she did it," Tower said. "Check out the backpack. It's not really a pack, it's a one-man harness to move someone down the mountain. That's how she moved them. She trained for this. Carrying heavy weights in that harness." In the video, the men saw her muscles grow taut and thick. Her shoulders were bulked up and she appeared to be able to easily carry a two-hundred-pound man. "She killed them, loaded them up and carried them to the body-dump site."

Mark David went into the bedroom and came back with a photograph. "Forensics is gonna be pissed I moved this, but I want this picture of her out there." In the photo, she is smiling and hugging a woman about the same age.

"Can I see that?" Tower tried to focus on the photograph. "I'm convinced she went to television as a sign that she is all-in. Whatever is her motive, she doesn't care anymore about getting it out in the open. The computer is waiting for us to see."

Mark David moved in another direction, going to the desk and pointing to something. "She left us a calling card."

Now Tower could see what Mark David was seeing. Tower's eyes went down to the floor for just a second, then back up to the object on the desk. Confirmation. David checked the numbers. "I know those numbers by heart. That's Sam's badge."

The weight of severe guilt crushed Tower's inner spirit and almost made him crumple to his knees. A whirlwind of past thoughts moved through him like a tornado. All things lined up. Past deeds came to the forefront and Tower felt his heart skip a beat. When he spoke, the words were soft, so he repeated himself to make sure he was heard. All of Tower's attention was directed to the photograph. "On the left is the fake Vera Rossin. And on the right..." Tower paused. "Now I know why she's here and why I'm a target."

## 55

Tower glanced out the window for just a second, then back at Mark David. "The woman on the right is Selene Carson. That has to be her sister."

Mark David brought the photograph closer to his face. "I remember the name. She was the one who was murdered. Stabbed several times. The defendant is on death row. She can't blame this on you because you were the one..." Now it was David's turn to pause.

"I was the one who had an affair with her. An affair with my own client." Tower was headed out the door. Three crime techs, all dressed in garb, booties, face masks and hoods, entered the apartment. David joined Tower. "You had nothing to do with her death."

"But I had everything to do with crossing the line with someone I was supposed to protect." Tower went down the stairs. David followed him to the ground floor.

"When Selene approached me, she wanted some information on a case involving a search for her ex-husband. She thought he was stalking her here in Stilton Bay. We tracked him down, and found he wasn't the one after her. As you know, the main suspect was stalking her all along. But in the process, I got too close to her. She was aggressive, came on to me and made it easy. I should have stepped away, but I didn't. Weak. Just plain weak."

"You and Shannon look happy now."

"But it almost cost me my marriage. Shannon is away at a conference, but she's also using this as an excuse for a trial separation. No phone calls until she comes back. If she comes back. Her rules."

"Understood."

A crime tech came up behind Mark David. The detective signaled for him to speak. They talked in quiet tones for about four minutes. Twice the tech looked over at Tower. The tech left and Tower got an update. "He says in her closet, there's stacks of news articles about Selene's murder. And more pictures of you."

"Okay. She wants me. So why take Sam?"

David took out his notepad. "What worries me is she could be using Sam to lure you into something. I'm hoping she makes contact with us. She could be saving a bullet for you Frank."

"I thought about that. It's clear this isn't the location for the murders of Kulis and Jed. And the money isn't here. She's got another place. A kill zone." Tower wiped a line of sweat from his brow. "She's been very bold about everything she's doing. Kinda like she's all in and doesn't care if we find her. Leaving Sam's badge up there. All that is for us. She's saying 'Come find me.' I just have to figure out where she is."

"Well, don't do it by yourself."

"She's on the run from the cartel, from the police, from the feds, and she doesn't care about the outcome. That means she is extremely dangerous."

"I have units watching the M.E.'s office in case she returns."

Tower shook his head. "She's not coming back. She's got it out for me and the town. No one is safe until you nab her up."

They were joined by a slender woman who flipped open her badge. She was wearing the familiar blue jacket with D.E.A. on the back. "Hi Frank. Detective, I'm JoJo Hardaway. D.E.A. We've never had a chance to meet before." She shook Mark David's hand. "Any word on Sam?"

David answered. "No. Not yet."

"I don't mean to add to your problems, but I thought you should know." She rested her hands on the large belt. "Rather than send you an email or try to call when you're so busy, I wanted to say this in person. We've got intelligence of a person you should watch out for. Someone we've been tracking for years. We've never been able to get a picture of him, just his handiwork once he leaves."

"Handiwork?" Tower said.

"Yeah. The guy is a specialist. Weapons. Torture. Gun suppresser. Whatever it takes. We just call him Mr. M, 'cause we don't know his name. But be careful. This guy is a hitman for the cartel. And as far as we know, he's now in Stilton Bay."

# 56

Lucas Park broke out into open laughter. Joy had overwhelmed him. He shook his fists in the air. The text message was short and to the point:

ONE MILLION DOLLARS

TONIGHT 11PM. DETAILS TO COME

His jaws were locked in a smile. 10:45 A.M. Plenty of time to get in touch with Cason Willow. Even though he was more than prepared, there was some work to be done. An escape plan out of Stilton Bay had to be finalized. How do you travel with that much money? The money could never go to a bank. Too risky, he reasoned. Park got on the computer and researched where to buy an RV. He could cut into the walls of the vehicle and stuff the inside with the money. And go anywhere.

Calm down, he thought. Too much adrenaline and he would be off his game. Four calls later, he had lined up two people willing to accept cash for a used RV. He just had to show up with the money. The first step would be to get the money. Next, buy the RV and retrofit the thing to his liking. He took off, headed to stores to buy the equipment needed to modify the RV.

He called Willow.

"You get it?" Park's excitement poured into his words.

"I got it." Willow sounded as enthused as a kid who missed out on Christmas.

"Think of it as the best opportunity possible," Park urged.

"I really don't want the money. I don't want any part of this."

"You're in it. We both are. That's too much money for one person to handle. I've got a rental van. We can put it there until we divide it up."

"What about any poison that might be on it?"

"We wear gloves and masks. We let the money sit for a couple of weeks and we should be just fine."

"I don't know."

"Listen. This is going to happen. Get it into your head. Tonight is the last drop. I know it. I'll pick you up around nine. Once we get the final details, we'll just keep an eye on the place. Get there in plenty of time."

"Okay. But I still say this is a mistake."

## 57

Frank Tower rubbed his forehead and dug fingers into his eyes before telling Lola. "We're headed to that rental place Jed used."

More than pleading, there was desperation in her voice. "You really need some sleep. You've been going at this for two days."

"No one is resting until we get Sam back."

The hour would soon be noon, straight-up. There was no hint of rain, giving the sky an open invitation to beat down anything moving outside with a Florida blast of sunshine. After twenty minutes of driving, Tower pulled into a space.

"Show me the way," he said.

For a hot second, Tower thought about calling Mark David. That idea dissipated with the notion he would be too busy tracking down leads on Sam, tending to poison victims and easing the guilt of Elly Kent. "If we find anything, we'll call out Mark."

Lola pulled out a key and stopped. She appeared shaken. "He gave me the keys to everything, but he didn't share why he didn't turn over something to the police."

"Don't worry. We will."

Lola turned the key. Tower followed her inside the townhouse. He flipped the light switch. Nothing.

"Oh, he never set up power for this place. Wanted to save money." She moved from the front living room to the one bedroom in the place.

"It's stifling in here." Tower sucked the stale air. "Did he ever open a window?"

"Never. Most times, I would stay in the car. This is where he kept all his files. Didn't want anything in his house. Just this place."

They entered the bedroom, only there was no bed. One wall was lined with metal filing cabinets. They opened each one, going through the voluminous files. For the next hour they looked at every file in the room.

Nothing.

Tower was glad he didn't call Mark David. A thought hit him. "Maybe what he did in his house, he did the same thing here."

Lola looked confused.

Tower went to the open side of the room and felt along the baseboard. With a little urging the board came loose. He pulled off the floorboard and found a small hole. Someone had carved out a small stash area. Tower reached inside.

He pulled out a thumbdrive and the paperwork with a list of dates.

Now it was decision-time. He could play the thing or call in Mark David. Again, he fell on the side to find out more first. "I've got a laptop in the car."

Tower made his way back to the front and opened the door. And stopped. In the working, roving eyes of a police officer, even a former cop, scenes, places, streets take up a place in the brain where information is stored and compared with other facts. For Tower, something did not look right. He looked left and right.

The bullet struck just above his head and a bit to the right. He slammed the door shut and pulled out his Glock. Tower yelled to Lola. "Get down. There's a shooter out there."

He could hear her moving into place near the heavy filing cabinets. He moved to a window and peered outside. A second shot smashed the glass pane. He was showered in glass bits. Tower did not want to just fire his weapon wantonly. Any number of innocent civilians could be in his line of fire. If the shooter approached, he wanted to be ready. Tower sized up his information. It seemed like there was one shooter who was on the street near his car. The suspect also was not moving forward. There was a slight upward angle on the bullet once it hit the door, making Tower think the person was not over six-feet-tall. Any attempt to leave through the front door was not an option. He pulled out his cell phone and called Mark David.

"Mark," Tower yelled into the phone. "We're being fired on. We're pinned down. I've got Lola with me at a rental place Jed had."

"More than one?" Mark David asked.

"I think it's just one person." Tower gave him the address.

"I'll get units rolling. You want to keep this line open?"

"I'll put the phone down. Get down here Mark." Tower put the phone on the dirt-gray carpet. He crawled on the ground and took up a position at another window. "Lola, you okay?"

"Yeah! Just get me out of here."

Tower took up a corner of the window, exposing the least amount possible of himself. He saw a figure. Just for a second. Tower didn't want to shoot unless he absolutely had to defend himself. Exactly two minutes and thirteen seconds later, Tower heard police sirens. The figure dropped down and was not seen again.

Seven police cars rolled up, officers getting out of their cars and drawing weapons. Most had long rifles. Overhead, a police helicopter circled the block. Mark David, gun aimed at the street, walked all the way up to the front door.

"C'mon out Frank."

Tower and Lola walked out of the townhouse. Tower's gun neatly tucked back in his pants. "Thanks," he said.

"You two okay?"

Tower looked at Lola and nodded yes.

"You get a look at them?"

"I think it was Wren, but I'm not sure. I think so. I think she was following Lola outside her house, and now here." He handed the flash drive over to Mark David. "This...is what Jed was supposed to turn over to you."

The detective stepped back for a moment, giving instructions for his people to step down, look for any witnesses and check in with his office for any signs of movement. He turned back to Tower.

"Man, you look terrible."

Lola hit him in the shoulder. "I've been trying to tell him. Look at his eyes. All red."

"No rest yet." Tower lamented.

"That's why someone was able to tail you without you catching them. You're off your game." Mark David walked back to his car and came back with a laptop. "Normally, I'd take this thumbdrive, let my techs look at it for a few days, get a report and store it. I don't have that kind of time." He inserted the drive. There were several files. Tower pointed to the top one on the monitor. The file just said evidence room. He opened the file. A video.

There was one person. Peona Wren. Her face was clear to the camera and undoubtedly, she had no idea the whole thing was being recorded. Wren was doing all of the talking. She was looking at another person off-camera, which had to be Kulis, but Wren was the star of the video. "Just like I promised. It's all here. My planning was perfect." The video showed a hand picking up a gym bag and handing it to Wren. She opened the bag, grabbed up a pile of cash and waived the cash at Jed. "You wouldn't have this without my input, just remember that. I made it happen." She shoved the money back down into the bag. "That's all of it. I don't want to risk another grab. Money for the police evidence room now belongs to us. The stink from this one will last a long time."

Wren picked up the bag and left.

Mark David closed the file. "Shows her direct involvement."

Tower said, "I can see why she wanted this file so bad."

"Lola, please come with me." David tucked the laptop under his arm. She had a surprised look on her face.

"Me?"

"Please come with me down to the station."

She marched off toward the unmarked car. "What's up, Mark? She's been with me the whole time."

"Not all the time. I'll tell you this. I shouldn't but here goes. We've checked Jed's financials. It seems he made two deposits, two months in a row totaling twenty thousand dollars."

"You think he was blackmailing Wren?"

"That's my guess. Jed played a part in this, along with his friend Kulis, who we believe actually stole the money then blamed you. He gives the money to Jed and he turns the bag over to Wren, but then decides to black-mail her. That would explain why she came back. That is, beside putting a target on your back." Tower handed Mark the piece of paper with the dates listed. "This was tucked away with the thumbdrive. I think if you check those dates against the financial statements from Kulis, my guess is they will match with deposits. Blackmail money from Peona. My client, Lola had nothing to do with this."

"Thanks, Frank. Now, please, go somewhere and get some sleep."

# 58

Frank Tower could not rest. The affair was eventually smoothed over with Shannon but on certain days, something would remind her of what had happened and their relationship teetered on the verge of collapsing. He told Lola that's why he was sleeping at his office and not home. While Lola slept in the back bedroom of the office, Tower found an old familiar place to crash in his surveillance van. Outside. His dreams were like rolling boulders. There were worries about Shannon, what could he do to find Sam, where was Vera now Peona. What if the cartel wanted to take revenge on the money-grabbers?

He woke up in a sweat. He tried to think of what Peona would do next. He entered the office and waited for Lola to come out of the bedroom so he could take a much-needed shower. She walked into the tiny kitchen, braless. Tower moved past her and took a shower. When he came out, she was ready for him.

"It's my turn to shower." Her smile was more than a smile. More of an invitation. "You're still wet. You want to join me?"

If there was an AA group for affairs and temptation, Tower would be a member. Sometimes the protective nature of his job, getting close or too close to a client, might bring him to the edge of doing something he would regret. Like now. In the few seconds before he answered, Tower saw how the last transgression ended. Affair, murder, an investigation, being cleared and a marriage on life support. Selene was more suggestive when they were together, shedding her clothes without hesitation. She wore him down and he knew there was absolutely no excuse for what he did. Before Lola took anything off, Tower spoke up. "One shower is enough. You just lost your boyfriend and I don't want to dishonor Jed's memory."

"I don't feel like showering anymore." She went to a sofa in the waiting room and sank into the cushions. Tower microwaved a dinner meal for them both and they ate in silence. A glance at his watch. 7:10 P.M. The next stop would be the police station and see if Mark David needed him somewhere.

# 59

Lucas Park was so giddy, he waited in the rental van rather than his apartment. 10:01 P.M. He was anxious to get moving. The back of the van was filled with empty roller suitcases. Cason Willow stood next to his car, pacing a few steps, then back. Park had his phone in his hand, ready. The next text came:

PLEASE PROCEED TOWARD THE BEACH

YOUR FINAL INSTRUCTIONS WILL COME IN TEN MINUTES

Park held the phone out the window showing Cason the text. He held up his own phone. Yes, he had the message as well. He got into his car and drove east toward the Atlantic. Willow did all he could to stay up with Park. Both cars were traveling right at the speed limit but not over.


Tower was given a place just outside the meeting room of the detective unit. The detectives met. Tower waited. He made Lola wait back at his office house and keep the doors locked. After several minutes, Mark David motioned for Tower to join them. The entire detective unit sat ready for more instructions.

Mark David said, "We're not sure if this is the lead we need but our IT director has something."

Randell Stemple stepped forward. "Detective David gave me an assignment days ago. We started tracking the GPS cell phone movements of anyone who touched any of the tainted money. We also put our street cameras on a quick alert. What we just saw in the last few minutes is this." Stemple clicked on a screen showing a grid of Stilton Bay Streets. There was a green dot moving east. "As you can see, this green dot shows a car moving at a good clip toward the ocean. We have determined this to be one Lucas Park. We have questioned him before. His wife is in the hospital after coming in contact with some of the money. From what we can determine, there is a car following Park. We do not know the identity of that second driver. Now Park is not in his regular car. We have surveillance that he is driving a van."

"Thank you." Mark David again took over the meeting. "We don't want the helicopter up yet, 'cause that might scare them off. We don't know where they will end up, so we want all of you to take assigned spots up and along A1A and wait. I will coordinate from here. Tower, you size this up and go where you think you can do the best. But everyone, please stay in touch with me. Is that clear?"

They all responded. Once the room cleared, Mark David singled out Tower. "Where are you going Frank?"

"Let me be your mobile trailer. I'll head east like everyone else, then make a decision."

"Okay." David handed Tower a police-authorized radio.

"Haven't had one of these in years."

"Keep in touch."

Tower drove east. He kept the radio conversations on low volume. Tower drove slowly, just like during the days when he patrolled the streets.

Lucas Park was two miles from the ocean when another text message lit up his cell phone. He tried to look and drive at the same time.

IN ONE BLOCK, PULL OVER

YOU WILL GET INTO A CAR PROVIDED FOR YOU

LEAVE YOUR CELL PHONE IN THE BASKET PROVIDED

DEVIATE FROM THESE INSTRUCTIONS AND THE MONEY IS GONE

Park pounded on the top of the dashboard. He kept hitting the dash when he pulled over and parked behind an old clunker. He tried to understand why he was being led on this way. He got out and waited for Cason Willow. "You get the message?" He yelled to Willow. "Why are they doing this?" Park was reluctant. He started looking for the bin. In front of them were two beaten down relics, cars from the 1970's.

Park tossed his phone into the bin. Willow looked around first, then tossed his phone.

"We have to move some equipment to these cars. And it looks like it's just us who got the texts." Park opened the door to the first car and grabbed the key, then opened up the trunk. He grabbed his mask and protective equipment and put them in the back seat. "I was going to put stuff in this trunk but I need the room for the money."

Willow paused. "Why are you so eager to do this, when there is a good chance we might find another body?"

"We don't know that."

Willow pressed him. "Think about it. Two money drops, two bodies. What makes you think we won't see another victim. That's one reason I don't want to do this."

"I told you, you don't have a choice. Stop now and I make sure the police know all about you."

"Why these cars?" Willow moved his gear.

"Simple. These cars were built before GPS. I get it. No cell phone, no new car. No way to track us." Park got behind the wheel. On the passenger seat, there was a sheet of paper. "This is it! Let's go." The paper had a new message. A final address.

Tower continued driving. The other units were in place and each officer checked in to report no movement. He parked and turned up the volume to his police radio. He heard communications telling anyone who gets near the cars, to stay back. There was no direct confirmation Park was involved in anything. Tower kept his Glock in the middle console while driving, rather than jammed into his hip, where he would have to fight to draw the weapon.


Stemple stepped hard in Mark David's direction. "We've got a problem. Both the car pings from towers show the cars moving out of Stilton Bay, headed to Fort Lauderdale."

Mark David rubbed his chin. "Do we have any street cams on them?"

"No." There was urgency in Stemple's voice.

"Tell one unit to move in. See where they are going."

Stemple dropped back and followed the directive.

Tower heard the communication. The male and female team of detectives in the unmarked unit 339 was told to get up close. Four minutes later, Detective Greena Wilson came on the radio. "You won't believe this, but both those cars are hooked up to tow trucks."

In the detective's office, Mark David shouted to the near empty room. "Dammit!"

He stood up from his desk just as Stemple entered the room again. Stemple stood by, as if waiting for instructions. David calmed down. "Tell them to stop the tow trucks. Find out what happened to the drivers. Find out what they can." He looked at the big map of Stilton Bay behind him. "It means we lost them."

Another ten minutes passed by on the clock when Wilson spoke up on the radio. "These drivers were sent a cash amount to pick up these cars. We found a cell phone in each car. They don't know anything, and I mean nothing about the drivers. They were just told to pick up these cars and drive them to Florida City."

There was a full forty-second pause before Mark David answered her. "Thank you. Impound the cars for evidence. You have their statements, release the tow truck drivers, but I want those cars. On our end, we'll see if we can pick up their trail."

Stemple looked scared to talk. "I tried doing that. Wherever those drivers got out, there are no street cameras. I don't think there are any businesses there either. Lucas Park and the other driver just disappeared."

Mark David picked up the phone and called Frank Tower.

"Hey Mark. They switched up cars? Listening to the radio."

"We have no read on where they are right now. I could really use your thoughts on where to find these two drivers. We know one is a person named Lucas Park. I can text you some info on him, driver's license photo, address, and other stuff. Process it and let me know. I'm going to have my folks go down the same route, see if they can find a witness on where this car exchange happened."

"Was he a main or a weak person of interest?"

"Weak. His wife is in the hospital, suffering from the money poison. When we interviewed him, he sounded legit, that she was the one who grabbed up the money. That's why we had an officer outside her hospital room. She was in a coma, woke up but she's still groggy. We really want to question her. But now, I'm beginning to think he was the guy who found the money, not her."

"No problem. I'll call you back."

"We are getting a court order to go through Park's text messages, phone records, his financials, everything."

"Gotcha. I'll be in touch. I'm going to try a hunch."

# 60

As Lucas Park drove, the move to the beat-up cars made sense to him. No cell phone, no computer-oriented car. And when they were done, they could burn the cars, and leave their personal cars out of the mix. Park was getting used to the little noises the car made, the different steering wheel and the worn-down brake pedal. In seven minutes, he was at the location on the paper.

Stilton Bay Cemetery.

Park got out of the car and studied the paper one more time. There were no directions on where to go now. Willow was parked behind him and was not getting out of his car.

"C'mon man!" Park was in the process of opening the rusty trunk, pulling out a roller suitcase.

Willow finally made it out from the driver's seat. "I want to make it clear I don't want any part of this."

"You're here 'cause I'm making you come. I'll blackmail your ass until the sun rises in the West. Get your suitcase and let's go."

Willow pulled out a suitcase and in his other hand, he had gloves and a mask. Both men wheeled up to the entry of the cemetery. While closed to cars because of after-hours, there was an open gate, leading to a walk path.

They looked around looking for a sign of where to go. Now masked-up in protection from poison fumes, they started searching.

"Look for an open area." The excitement picked up in Park's voice. His head snapped left to right and back looking for the right location.

In the darkness, the gravestones stood like quiet witnesses, each with a different story of lives lived and the passing of a person. Willow slowed down, gathering in the names and dates. "I don't like this. Let's go back." His voice was just a bit muffled coming through the mask.

"Keep going."

They stopped. Off to their left, there was a clearing under a tree. Park moved from the path to the grass, pulling the suitcase over the now bumpy turf. Both looked for any sign of cash.

The clearing was lined in shadow. Neither man had a flashlight. Park moved into the middle of the space and found a bench. This had to be a respite for bereaved parties to sit and reflect on a life lost.

Sitting on the bench was a man.

His eyes were closed. His hands were behind his back and might have been tied; Park did not know. There was a gag in his mouth and a scratch on his forehead as though he had been in a fight.

"Bingo!" Park shouted. "The money must be on him." Park knew the routine. The money had to be stuffed down inside the shirt, but for this amount, something was wrong.

Willow froze and did not move. Park moved in and started to pat him down. That's when the figure on the bench opened his eyes.

"No way." Willow took a step backward.

"Get in here," Park said over his shoulder.

Woozy at first, the man focused on Park and though he could not speak, the fiery eyes were enough. The man wriggled but could not break free of the ropes tying him to the bench.

"This guy is alive," Willow was about to turn and run.

"Don't move," Park ordered. After trying unsuccessfully to speak, the man glowered. Park yelled, "Where's the money?"

"He doesn't have any money?" Willow looked both surprised and curious.

"It must be here." Park moved three paces. There was a note on the bench. Park read the short message and held up the paper to Willow, waiting for him to come closer.

"They want us to kill him?" Willow spoke each word like a man contemplating the consequences if they got caught.

Park sized up the man sitting in front of him. "I don't see any money. Why kill him if there's no money?"

There was no mistaking the sound of a gunshot. A piece of the bench broke off in splinters and Willow's body snapped down into a crouched position. Park looked for a shooter. Out of the backdrop of cemetery markers and ghoulish bends in the foliage, a voice. Just the voice.

"Kill him or there's no money."

"And all this time, I thought we were dealing with a man. A woman's voice." Now Park looked for her.

"Around his neck is a key. A key to the mausoleum behind you. The money is in there. Look on the ground. You'll find two knives. Kill him and you're both rich men."

Willow saw them. There was just enough light to flash and glint off the metal of the long knives. "We have to leave him."

Willow shook his head. "You think she's gonna let us leave here after killin' this guy? We don't have much choice here." He whispered, "She's going to kill all of us. Don't you get it?"

Park shouted to the arrangements of grave markers. "Why don't you kill him? We don't have any quarrel with this guy?"

The answer came back. "Dead or alive, you both want the money. How far are you willing to go? You have thirty seconds."

"Or what?" Park asked.

"Twenty-five seconds."

Park reached for one of the knives. The man on the bench squirmed and wriggled, stretching the limits of the ropes in an effort to get free. The veins in his neck bulged like cables. Park tossed the other knife at Willow. "You're a part of this."

"I can't do it."

Park pleaded. "You have to. Or we die."

"Fifteen seconds," the voice screamed.

Willow stared at the knife. Park picked up his blade and moved closer to the man on the bench.

"Stop right there!" Frank Tower moved in slow, aiming his Glock at the closest threat to the tied-up man. Lucas Park.

"But you don't understand," Park explained.

"I'm Frank Tower, working with Stilton Bay Police. Put the knife down. Now!" Tower held his ground, waiting for a response.

"Thanks for joining us," the voice sounded calm.

Tower turned in the direction of the blue-black shadows. "I wasn't sure, but I thought I'd come here. Your sister is buried here, isn't she? Selene?"

"You remembered. I was wondering if you could work it out."

"Stop this game you're playing, Peona. Step out so I can see you."

A shot knocked the radio off Tower's belt. Three inches more and he would be paralyzed. The rocket noise of the bullet being fired made Tower move behind a tall headstone for cover. The radio was in pieces. He did not want to reach for his phone just yet. Willow and Park were face-down on the ground. "Peona, stop shooting." Tower then turned his attention to the three men. "You two. The man on the bench is a police officer. Move away from him now! That's an order!"

Another shot. The bullet chipped a piece off the headstone. Firing wildly into the night was not Tower's goal. He refrained from using his weapon unless she moved out into the light. Willow complied. He inched along the ground, getting back from the man tied-up. Park tightened his grip on the knife.

Just when Tower turned to look for Peona, Park lunged for the man on the bench. He reached for the key ring and used his knife to cut the thin necklace of rope around the man's neck.

Park tucked the key close to his chest and ran for the mausoleum. A bullet kicked up the dirt near Park's feet as he ran for the door. The next shot hit another section of the bench, only closer to the target. Willow grabbed his knife and dove at the man on the bench. The first bullet missed Willow. The second nipped a piece of his left shoulder. From Tower's angle, the shot would have hit the seated man. Willow tore at the ropes with his knife.

Tower fired four shots in the direction of the gunfire. The shots gave

Willow a chance to cut the ropes. Once freed, Sam Dustin pulled Willow behind two grave markers.

Lucas Park used the key and opened the door. With the gun blasts ringing in the near distance, he found the money. Stacks of money. He had no suitcase. His shirt was already fitted to accept large amounts of money. Park started stuffing stacks of bills inside his shirt, his pockets, and down his back. Everywhere he could think of stashing the cash. He resembled a man overstuffed with too many meals. Only Park was feeding on money. He waited until there was a moment to run and took off, moving far to his left, leaving the clearing and running as fast as a middle-aged man could run with thousands of dollars ballooning in his clothing.

He made it all the way back to his car. He got inside and drove off. Clean away.

Tower yelled to Peona. "It's over. Someone is going to report these gunshots. Give it up."

She moved out of the charcoal mist and into the open. Her gun was at her side, like she was in the old west, ready to draw. "You have one last chance, Frank. We do this my way. My way or I start shooting at those two men."

Tower put his Glock into the holster. They stood there, like two gunslingers ready to duel it out at high noon. Only this was a cemetery, late at night.

"Why are you doing this, Peona?"

"You know why Frank."

"What happened to your sister was horrible. A terrible thing. But I didn't have anything to do with her death."

"She trusted you. She came to you. You could have protected her. That's why I came after you. Planted the gun, planted evidence. Everything. I wanted this entire city to suffer. These stupid people jumped at the money! Right off the dead. And the poison got some of them. I'm glad. Draw! Frank."

Sam Dustin first moved in Tower's direction, stopped, and instead pressed his hand into the wound in Cason Willow's shoulder. Limit the bleeding.

"Kulis Barney was blackmailing you."

"I was in on the evidence theft. Barney recorded the whole damn thing. I looked for that thumbdrive. Then came the blackmailing. You're wasting time. Draw."

"But then you decided to kill him instead."

"I've done a lot of bad stuff. Killing him was not one of those things. He deserved it."

"And Jed? He wasn't doing anything."

"He kept the thumbdrive from me. Wouldn't give it up. Had to go." She shook her right hand, loosening her fingers over her weapon. The sleeves to her shirt were cut at the shoulders, showing her muscled arms.

Both of them held steady, eyes checking each other.

Tower waited until she moved first. She drew her weapon and fired. The hot round was just above Tower's head. Tower dropped to the ground and out of her line of vision. He used the moments on the ground to get closer and then he sprang, jumping into her chest, sending both of them to the ground. She hit her head on a rock, making her dazed and a bit confused. Tower moved in and took her gun, tossing it in the direction of Sam Dustin.

Tower reached for his cell phone and called Mark David.

# 61

Sixteen Stilton Bay police cars, lights flashing, ringed the entrance to the cemetery. Peona sat in the back of one car. Four officers guarded her.

Tower sighed. "How's the man who was shot?"

Mark David kept his eyes on Peona. "His name is Cason Willow. From what Sam tells me, the guy probably saved his life. Took a bullet for him. Claims he was forced into this."

"You believe him?"

"Get this, he brought one of those tape recorders and got this guy Lucas Park to admit everything. All their conversations were recorded."

"Where is Park now?"

"We've got several units looking for him."

One of the officers approached them. "She's saying she's not feeling well, that she's about to get sick. Wants to see a doctor."

Tower asked, "You trust her?"

Mark David reached for his police radio. "I don't want some just-passed-the-bar attorney to say we denied her medical assistance. Willow is already on the way to the hospital. They can come back and take one more."

David used his radio to work up a detail to follow the fire rescue truck to the emergency room. In less than three minutes, another fire unit arrived. The officer on her door, let her out. He walked her, in cuffs, to the doors of the rescue unit. Peona stopped right at the door and turned to Tower and Mark David. "I'll beat this, you watch! I'll figure a way to..."

She never finished her sentence.

Peona's face jolted back an inch. Her jaw locked in place and a red dot of blood appeared on her forehead. A line of crimson dripped down from the dot, forming a red trail leading to her left eye and spilling over the tip of her nose. The shot was silent. She stood there, eyes still open, dying, standing erect. Every officer there hit the ground, weapons aimed at what might be the shooter's direction.

"Sniper!" Someone yelled.

All guns were pointed and ready, but there was no target to focus on. Tower moved toward Peona, but he wasn't fast enough to get her behind cover.

The second shot landed squarely in the middle of Peona's chest, ripping a piece of her blouse. Small at first, a circle of blood spread out in an expanding circle until her entire front was covered.

Paramedics rushed to Peona, catching her as she collapsed to the ground. The fire rescue unit rushed her to the hospital, but she was gone.

Tower saw one leaf move forty yards away and then the leaf was still.

Officers searched for the next two hours and found nothing. Whoever the shooter was, he picked up his shell casings. Upon inspection, the area looked to be swept, leaving no trace of footprints or knee impression. No cigarette butts or handprints in the dirt. A professional hit.

Tower tried to console Mark David. "You did what you could. If they wanted to get to her, it would have been here or in the jail."

"Still, she was my hold. That second shot was to make sure she was down. Doubt if we'll ever find the shooter."

"Where are you headed?"

"Just one thing, Frank. Got to locate Lucas Park."

# 62

Lucas Park snuggled up in the humid layers of roof insulation and tried to think about other things than the rising temperature of the condominium attic. He managed to evade two detectives in the parking lot, dropped off the money to his condo unit and used the management ladder to reach the inner matrix of wooden rafter beams. Park wiped away some rat droppings and leaned up against a truss. He had pulled up the ladder with him. There was a cut on his right ankle from moving away from the beat-up car when he pushed the thing into a nearby pond. All he had to do now was count up the money, double-check the rental car was still okay, and buy a new burner phone.

Now, he waited.

He had to stay still or the couple in the unit below would hear him. Just after noon, Park cracked open the roof door and looked out. The parking lot looked quiet. He eased the ladder down, walked two flights down to the eighth floor and entered his apartment. Without hesitation, he tore off his shirt and went into the shower. When he finished drying himself, Park went out into the living room to check on his money again.

The cash was not there.

"Hello Lucas." Joni Park came out of the kitchen, moving about with a limp.

"When did you get home?"

"They tried calling you all evening and into the night. Where have you been?"

"Joni, where is the money that was on the coffee table. A lot of money."

"I lost a kidney, but the doctor says I should recover and do just fine."

"Joni, where is my money?"

"I will need some therapy, but they will be calling to set that up."

"Where is my fucking money!" His eyes bulged with anger.

"Aren't you glad to see me? Not once have you asked how I was doing. Not once."

"The only thing I care about right now is the money that was on the table. Again, where is my money?"

"The nurses say it was a miracle that I woke up. A miracle. Isn't that great, Lucas?"

Park rocketed from the living room to the bedroom and back again looking for the stacks of cash. "I had them all lined up. Nice neat stacks. A lot of money." Finally, he got up close to her and balled up his fist. "Where is the money? What did you do with it?"

"Oh that. I packed it up and moved it."

"Where!"

"It's out there. I put it out on the balcony."

Park's eyes lasered to the balcony. A bead of sweat broke through his receding hairline and rolled over the bumpy forehead. "Out there?"

"Yep. I figured you wanted to get it out of the house. So, I moved it."

Park slowly rolled open the sliding glass door. "I don't see anything. Where did you put it?"

"Look over the railing. It's there."

Park stepped out onto the balcony like a man testing thin ice. "You say the railing?"

"Yep."

He conjured up all the time he had spent weakening the railing. Park moved as slow as he could until he reached out with both hands and grabbed the railing. He bent over the top rail and looked down. A rope, tied to the bottom of the railing, led to an enormous bag. Park was able to tell his cash was neatly stored in the holding bag. He reached down with both hands, untied the bag and started pulling up the haul. His knee moved against the railing and Park heard something snap. The railing, free from the bag, fell out of the mounting holes and dropped eight stories down. He heard a loud clang as the metal hit the surface below. Park tried to hang on, but his momentum propelled him over too much and he was now grabbing the balcony with just his left hand by clutching a small jagged piece of metal left behind from the railing. The money bag was heavy and Park felt the drag pull on his hand.

"Joni, honey. I need some help out here. Help!"

Joni Park ambled out onto the balcony. "Ya know, it is true what they say."

"Say what Joni? I need some help. Pull me back in! Now!"

"It's very true. They say when you're in a coma, sometimes you can hear what people are saying." She stepped closer to the desperate Lucas. Her words were soft yet forceful. "I heard every word you said, Lucas. Every word."

"Joni honey, please. I didn't mean it. Please help me out."

"All you have to do is let go of the money. Let it go, Lucas. And help yourself back up."

There was a new-found confidence in her voice. Fear of him had evaporated like drops on a hot Florida sidewalk. Her words were calculated and blooming with an inner strength and adrenalin that made her body shake. "When I heard all that, made me think."

"I worked hard for this money. Help me, Joni. My grip is coming..."

"Yep. Heard it all. It's time Lucas to help yourself."

His grip on the wall gave way.

Lucas fell from the balcony. When he dropped, the money bag opened up. One-hundred and one-thousand-dollar bills floated down like a glittering cloud of green butterflies. The money flittered at different speeds, all drifting down, stacking up like a pile of snowflakes. Park kept reaching for the balcony, but he was moving at a speed he could not conceive, arms flailing at the air, at times grabbing for the wafting bills. When he did hit the ground moments later, some of the money dropped softly and settled into the growing pool of blood near his head. Still, in his last few seconds of life as he descended, Park heard just two words from his wife of eight years.

Just two words.

She cupped her hands and as loud as she could, she yelled. "Die bitch!"

# 63

Frank Tower waited on the outside of the police crime tape for Mark David to finish checking the scene where Lucas Park landed. Three times David started in Tower's direction only to turn around and converse again with the crime techs. Almost thirty minutes passed before he made it to Tower.

"They wanted to keep the money where it was and take a photograph, but the wind won't cooperate. They're picking up the money now. We estimate just over one million. Park wouldn't have gotten very far."

Mark David looked around at the crowd trying to gather on the west side of the scene. "Would you believe it, all that money and no one wanted to take any. Guess they're still concerned it might be poisonous."

"Park's wife?"

"She's fine, physically. Apparently, no poison on the money. Two people say she yelled something when he fell, but they couldn't make out what she was saying. She's upset at the whole thing. Said she tried to catch him but couldn't get to him in time. We'll take her statement and let her grieve. But some neighbors did say they thought they saw Lucas Park messn' around with the railing for months."

"How's the other guy from the shooting. Cason Willow?"

"He's at the hospital. Took a through and through in the shoulder. Sam

Dustin is with him. Says Willow jumped in front of him. Took the hit. Sam's waiting for him to come out of surgery, wake up and thank him."

"So, no charges for him?"

"I'll leave that up to the state attorney, but Willow had that tape recording. Along with helping Sam, I think he's in the clear."

"Mark, how's Sam doing?"

"He's okay. He's more embarrassed how she took him down. Vera, or Peona, suckered him in, saying she had some good information. Then, she pulled out a stun gun. His mind was blank after that. But, he's planning to thank you in person for showing up when you did."

Tower said, "Even with a lab coat, you could see she was muscular."

"We're still going over the videos on her laptop. There's more vids of her going back three years with that back brace carrying people around. We also found a table where she transferred your prints. I'm guessing she got them from her sister's old apartment. There were some bloody bills, some clear tape to transfer the prints. It's all there." Mark David took two quick steps and grabbed an errant one-hundred-dollar bill caught up in a gust. A crime tech ran over to get it from him. "In her drug lab, we found the old plans to steal the money headed to our evidence room. She planned it, brought in Kulis and Jed. They got their cut, turned around and blackmailed her." Mark David rubbed his chin. "Frank, explain to me how you knew to go to the cemetery?"

"It was a hunch. When Selene died, the cemetery staff got an anonymous donation of forty-thousand dollars for the mausoleum. I just thought it would make natural sense for Peona to honor her sister's memory by doing the last murder there."

"Everything was in her drug lab. Wasn't far away. Less than a mile from the cemetery. We got all kinds of chemicals, tons of equipment, but I don't think we will ever know the recipe for what she used on the money. The bomb squad is working on it. It's where we believe she killed Kulis and Jed. We found blood."

Tower asked, "How did she get their phone numbers for the texts?"

"From what the tech guys are saying, she paid for a phone listing. She was very specific in that she apparently only wanted numbers from Stilton Bay. It doesn't take much to investigate the numbers for an address connected to the phone, search them out and see how they live. It would have taken months."

Mark David said, "The hospital reports just one person is in ICU. They've got a good handle on how to treat everyone and I think we've turned the corner on this. And by the way, we're invited to the mayor's office for an official thank you. And that includes you."

"I think I'll pass." Tower watched a cab arrive. Lola Henderson paid the driver and walked toward Tower.

"And we found something else." Mark David gathered Tower in so only he could hear. "She liked trophies. She had them all laid out on a shelf. Even had a light shining down on them."

"Trophies?" Tower asked.

"The four bullet fragments she dug out of the brains of her two victims. She wanted them." He shook his head.

Tower said, "Sounds like she's been planning this for a long time."

Mark David said, "Thanks for the thumbdrive. Just part of the puzzle."

Tower's phone buzzed. He motioned for Lola to wait for a second. On the phone was Jo Jo Hardaway. "I'm glad you got it wrapped up."

Tower tapped the phone. "Let me put this on speaker so Mark can hear it."

Jo Jo coughed for a second. "We got nothing on the hitman. Far as we know, and it's tough to verify, but we think he's gone. So, now we have to track him down again."

"We'll work on it." Mark David said.

"In case you're wondering," Jo Jo started. "With all this tainted money, I think that's why the cartel didn't move to take it back. Call it a business write-off. Be safe."

"Thanks Jo Jo." Tower put away the phone. Mark David left him to oversee the removal of Lucas Park's body.

"You okay?" Lola blocked the sun out of her eyes.

"I'm okay."

She moved in close and reached for his face with her hands. "You look like you need a shower. You never got a chance to join me."

"I'm good."

"I can fix you a meal, give you a back rub. Kiss your tired eyes and won't let you leave the house."

"I can do all that." A woman was stepping hard in Tower's direction.

Lola squinted. "And just who are you?"

"You can take off. I'm Frank Tower's wife."

## 64

The stay at the beach hotel was for two days. After five days, they were still there. They looked out over the Atlantic. The water was rolling in easy, its soft waves filled with bait fish. Ocean fingers of azure and purple moved in and reached up on the shore leaving lines of foam. The sand was warm to the touch. Shannon Tower's toes easily dug into the smooth beach. Her footprints in the sand were erased by turquoise blue water with each arriving wave.

He reached over and took her hand. "I kept my promise. I only called you once during this whole thing."

"I know. I kept reading what was going on. I thought you would call right away."

Tower kicked at a shell in the sand. "All that time away. Did that help you?"

Shannon wiped salt spray from her golden-toned skin. "When I went to the conference, it did give me a chance to think about us. About you. And whether I wanted to continue to let what happened with Selene, be a small wall between us. Or divide us. But I decided it's time to go forward. With you. And so, I came back."

They walked without talking. Finally, Shannon stopped. "That woman,

Lola, I just wanted to let you know that I trusted you. But she told me you were a gentleman."

Tower took her hand again.

A line of seagulls in fighter wing formation, moved past them heading north. Three boats, one sporting fishing poles, cruised south, each leaving a V-pattern of wavy action on the water. The deeper water in the Atlantic was always darker. Mother Nature kissed the shoreline with a breeze much cooler than just minutes earlier. Miles out, a rain cloud was dumping drops too far to be anyone's concern. Three fishing boats looked like toys on the ocean. One could imagine the boat captains looking for floating objects in the water, then drop lines. Some of the best tasting fish clung to areas near things in the water. One just had to look.

Something was cutting the waves and surfacing for just a few scant moments, then dropping out of sight. A cacophony of bird sounds floated on the air and mixed with the constant ripple of waves. An orchestra of life played out for those venturing out from the condos and mansions of Stilton Bay.

Tourists were back and all was peaceful.

Hundreds were up and down the beach, some running into the water, others on blankets. Each person creating moments to remember, basking in the fresh goodness that comes with Florida sunshine.

And no one paid any attention to the couple of Frank and Shannon Tower walking in the sand.

## INVESTIGATION ENVY
### Frank Tower Mystery #4

**Frank Tower is back to investigate a serial killer full of rage, envy, and cold-blooded cruelty in this thrilling fourth installment of the Frank Tower Mystery Series.**

The first body is discovered at the city park, arranged in an unnatural position, eyes wide open.

Inside the body, police find a thumb drive with a countdown clock until the next victim is killed—and a demand to inform PI Frank Tower about the murder.

The victim's best friend hires Tower to investigate, but with limited clues and stubborn resistance from the police, he's in for his toughest case yet. Soon, several other victims are discovered in public areas across the city, each body containing a similar thumb drive. Each time, the countdown clock shows less time to stop the next murder.

And then a chilling discovery forces Frank to make an impossible choice.

When the clock runs out, will he beat the killer at his own game...or lose the ones he loves the most?

**Get your copy today at
severnriverbooks.com/series/frank-tower-mystery-thrillers**

# AUTHOR'S NOTE

The location for my book, Florida, is a natural beauty of ocean-kissed beaches and to the west, the wild and exotic Everglades. The state is an ideal place for my characters to delve into mystery and intrigue. However, the city of Stilton Bay, with a picturesque main street, downtown park, the beach and its infamous red-light district called T-Town, are all products of my imagination.

# ABOUT THE AUTHOR

For many years, Mel Taylor watched history unfold as he covered news stories in the streets of Miami and Fort Lauderdale. A graduate of Southern Illinois University, Mel writes the Frank Tower Private Investigator series. He lives in a community close to one of his favorite places – The Florida Everglades. South Florida is the backdrop for his series.

Sign up for Mel's reader list at
severnriverbooks.com/authors/mel-taylor